EIGHT DAYS ON PLANET EARTH

Also by Cat Jordan

The Leaving Season

EIGHT DAYS

* * *

on PLANET

EARTH

CAT JORDAN

HARPER TEEN
An Imprint of HarperCollinsPublishers

HarperTeen is an imprint of HarperCollins Publishers.

Eight Days on Planet Earth
Copyright © 2017 by Cat Jordan
All rights reserved. Printed in the United States of America.
No part of this book may be used or reproduced in any manner
whatsoever without written permission except in the case of
brief quotations embodied in critical articles and reviews. For
information address HarperCollins Children's Books, a division of
HarperCollins Publishers, 195 Broadway, New York, NY 10007.
www.epicreads.com

ISBN 978-0-06-257173-1
17 18 19 20 21 PC/LSCH 10 9 8 7 6 5 4 3 2 1
❖
First Edition

For my dad, John,
who will always be a star

Remember to look up at the stars and not down at your feet. Try to make sense of what you see and about what makes the universe exist. Be curious.

—*Stephen Hawking*

The Universe makes sense.
We're just too small to understand.

—*DJ Jones*

I want to believe.

—*Fox Mulder*

DAY ONE

6:02 A.M.

I kick off the covers way too early, still on school time since the year ended just a few days ago. Stumble down the back staircase to the kitchen to make coffee and walk Ginger, our runty white Lab.

The stone floor is cool under my bare feet, and the whole house feels eerily silent. Something's off, or maybe it's just me. Coffee will help.

Our kitchen used to be an attached shed that my granddad renovated in the seventies. It was pretty modern back then, but nothing's been updated since he died. We've got one of the first microwaves ever created and a Mr. Coffee drip pot from the late twentieth century.

I'm probably the only guy I know who can make coffee in his sleep: water, filter, a hundred scoops of Maxwell House (because it's good to the last drop). Press the button and we're good to go. That's when I take Ginger out for a walk. By the time we're back, the coffee's done and I feed Ginger and . . .

Ginger isn't there.

Her doghouse, which I painted red like Snoopy's when I was eight, is empty.

"Ginger! Ginger! Here, girl!" I whistle for her and clap my hands and probably wake up the entire street, but she doesn't come to me.

"Ginger! Ginger!" I hold my breath and listen for her paws rustling in the bushes or her panting as she clambers up the short hill from the woods. All is quiet. Ginger has run away before, but she always returns, usually right around mealtime.

I clap my hands a few more times and whistle as I walk around the outside of the house. Maybe she's stuck somewhere, trying to crawl after a ball or a bird? The bushes and trees are still, and the driveway where my granddad built a basketball hoop is empty.

The open garage door catches my eye. It should be closed. I should be looking at a sign that says *Jones Family Farm* in fat orange letters painted across the faded wood.

I take a few steps closer and find Ginger lying on the

concrete floor of the garage in the spot where my dad's pickup is usually parked. Her front paws are crossed with her head resting on top of them.

"Hey, girl," I croon. "Whatcha doin'?"

Her brown eyes are wide as she seems to shake her head. *Darned if I know.*

The pickup. Where's Dad's pickup truck? Mom's Honda is in its place, but there's only a sad-looking Labrador retriever with a streak of gold down her back sprawled on the oil-stained concrete.

My heart sinks to my stomach. It feels wrong, this empty garage. Ginger knows it too.

Mom . . .

By the time I get inside, my mother is sitting at the round wooden table in the breakfast nook, drinking some of the coffee I made. She has a smile on her face, which tells me she doesn't know yet about the empty garage.

"Good coffee." She lifts her mug—an oversize ceramic thing that holds twice the usual amount of liquid—and nods. She drinks at least three of these every morning before work.

"Thanks."

She isn't dressed in her normal work scrubs. She's wearing the pink shorts and tank top she likes to sleep in, along with a thin cotton robe and flip-flops. Her hair isn't ready for work either; her brown pixie cut sticks up all over her head, like she's gotten an electric shock.

She waves a hand at the coffeepot. "Grab some more of that for me, would you?"

I pour myself a cup and then refill hers. Black. No sugar. Two sugars for me.

"Sit, Matty, sit," she urges. There's an edge in her voice, a tone warning me something is coming. My mother's hand slides into the front pocket of her robe, and I hear the *scritch-scritch* sound of her nails on paper.

"What's that?" I aim my gaze at her pocket.

Mom's eyes flicker from me to her lap and back again. She takes out a crumpled envelope and lets it sit on her thigh for a very long moment. Her fingers tremble and her foot bounces nervously, the plastic sandal making a snapping sound against her bare skin. "Your dad . . ."

"He's gone," I say, but it sounds like a question. "Is that . . . is that what you want to tell me?"

There's a hitch in her breath when she sighs. "I don't think . . . well, I don't know for sure, but—no, no, I *do* know. He's—yes, he's gone."

The *scritch-scritch* again draws my gaze. "And that's . . . a note from him? Did he leave us—you, I mean, did he leave you a note?"

"Matty—"

I grab it from my mom's hand. "'Dear Lorna . . .'" That's my mom. "'I'm sorry, but Carol and I . . .'" And that's all I see before Mom snatches it back. Not that I need to see any

6

more. I know who Carol is: the wife of my uncle Jack, my dad's brother. Like my mother, Jack is ten years younger than my dad, and Carol is ten years younger than Jack, which makes Dad running off with Carol . . . really pathetic.

"Well, that's that." I hear a quaver in my voice and swallow to clear it.

"We don't know that." My mom looks both too young and too old. Cheeks sprinkled with freckles and gray hairs at her temples. "We don't know what will happen."

"Yeah, sure."

"He could . . ." Her words hang in the humid air. She takes a long gulp of coffee as her eyes dart around the kitchen. Does she really want him back? Seriously? A guy with no steady job who'd rather tweet and write blog posts all day? A guy who let his own family business wither and die because he couldn't be bothered to care?

I stand abruptly and the table shifts. "I gotta eat." At the sound of "eat," Ginger whines. "Oh crap, I forgot." I bend down and rub the dog's neck. "Sorry, girl. I got your breakfast. Hang on."

Mom waves her mug. "You got that, yeah?"

"Yeah, no worries."

"And your breakfast too?"

"What am I, ten? I can make breakfast for myself."

She cocks an eyebrow. "You sure?"

"Uh, which one of these things is the toaster again?" I walk up to the refrigerator. "This one? Is this it?" I tap the microwave. "Oh no, it's this one, right?"

My mom smiles for a split second and then presses her lips together. "I gotta get ready for work. I leave Ginger and Mr. Coffee in your capable hands." She finishes her mug silently, not looking at me. A minute later, I feel her hand rest on my shoulder as I'm pulling down a bag of kibble. She's about a foot shorter than me, petite framed, and tough. She doesn't look it but my mom is one kick-ass mother. "Have a good day. It'll be okay."

I shrug off the implication that my dad leaving would in any way impact my day, week, and/or life. "Well, duh, it's summer. It'll be great."

She holds my gaze for a long moment, and in that time, I try to read what she's thinking. Are we on the same wavelength about Dad? This isn't a big deal, right? We're not devastated, are we? Our eyes meet and she suddenly glances away as if she's said too much, projected too many feelings. "Yes, then, good."

She looks like she might need a hug, but we're not real touchy-feely in the Jones family. It would be weird for me to offer her one. Instead I salute her as she walks out the door.

I scoop out some kibble for Ginger, wondering about the letter in my mom's pocket. What else did my dad write? Is there anything in there about me? Not that I care. He's always had his own shit going on that had nothing to do with us. Maybe now he'll finally be happy.

I hear my mom upstairs in her room above the kitchen,

padding lightly from dresser to closet to bed. It hasn't been easy being David James Jones's wife; she's had to hold the family together for a while now. Maybe she'll finally be happy too.

12:04 P.M.

I wait until noon to text Brian. He and Emily are late risers. In fact, the entire Aoki family is on a different schedule from us. Late to bed, late to rise. Maybe because we used to be farmers, we're always up with the sun.

Yo, meet me? I text him.

Yo, yep is the reply. We don't really need more than that.

We meet where we usually do, at the back of the old drive-in behind the huge plaster screen. On weekends the place is used for a swap meet, but during the week it's empty. Brian and I have been hanging out there since we were kids. We rode regular banana seat bikes and BMXes until we turned fourteen and got cheap scramblers. For the past three years, we've been tearing up the dirt like pros.

Ha. No.

One time, we set up a ramp using some raw lumber and concrete blocks we found on the side of the road and dragged to the drive-in. Without any training or practice whatsoever, Brian attempted to jump off the ramp. I never saw so much blood pour out of one nose. His face connected with the concrete like it was a cream-filled doughnut. *Splat*.

The Aokis moved into the stone house at the very end of our rural road when Brian was a baby and his sister, Emily, was barely a toddler. As the only boys on the entire street, we became fast friends as soon as we could talk. Em hung out with us too, but she was kind of an honorary guy, plus she could drive before us so that gave her bonus points.

"Yo," Brian calls to me when he rides up to the movie screen. He's wearing cutoff cargo pants and a black T-shirt that billows out over his stomach. Brian has always been conscious of his weight. His dad got diabetes when he was forty and he's been hammering at Brian ever since to lose weight and eat right.

Please. Those cargo pants are stuffed with Almond Joys, not grapefruit.

Well, Almond Joys and weed. He takes a couple of quick puffs off a joint and offers it to me. I shake my head and he shrugs, taking another toke. "Your loss."

"Did you ride with that thing lit?"

"Yeah, maybe."

I laugh. "Dude."

"I'm super skilled."

"Sure. It's how you got a D in every class—"

He punctuates the air with the joint. "Not true. I got a C in history."

History at our high school is a joke. No one has ever failed. Even the worst student—and arguably that was Brian—never got anything less than a C-minus. We're entering our senior year with dueling crappy averages, me because I'm bored out of my mind and Brian because, well, he's not dumb but he'd rather smoke dope than study.

"What are we doing today?" he asks, shading his eyes with his hand as his gaze roams the empty drive-in. The place is filled with leftovers from a bygone era: metal rods planted in the dry earth, bent and crushed by wind and rain and probably me and Brian when we were younger; dead speakers, the type that clipped to car windows, used to hang by their wires but disappeared a few years ago. The snack bar is the last original structure still intact, and that's only because the swap meet organizers need a designated smoking area.

"I dunno. What do *you* wanna do?"

"Lake?"

"What, to swim?" At best, my pudgy stoner friend might float, but there's no way he's going to exercise on his own.

"Swim? Dude, please." He sucks in another drag from the joint and holds it in his lungs. "Just hang," he ekes out before exhaling the smoke. The sweet smell of it immediately evaporates into the dusty air.

"Hang?" I know what he wants to do at the lake: stare at the girl lifeguard he has a crush on. "Like, get a tan? Is that what you wanna do? Or maybe rent a boat? No!" I snap my fingers. "Paddleboard." I mime rowing with an invisible oar, wiping my brow of imagined sweat.

"Fuck you, Jones."

"Go on, say it."

"What."

"Say her name. Go on." I poke his chest with two fingers. "Mir. An. Da." I poke him again, and his butt slips off the seat of the dirt bike. I lean in and whisper in his ear, "You know you want her."

His cheeks purple with embarrassment. "You're a douche." He holds up the joint, pinches off the end between his fingernails, and tucks it into the front pocket of his cargo shorts. "Don't ask. You're not getting any."

I shrug. "Don't care." Jeez, so he likes a girl.

And I guess because of their shared DNA or whatever, I'm suddenly thinking of Emily.

Brian's sister has their mom's heart-shaped face with cheeks that dimple when she smiles; auburn hair she keeps in a ponytail most of the time; curves hidden under Levis and an Eagles sweatshirt. A few of us guys know she's got a killer bod, but she's constantly in motion. Field hockey in the fall, dive team in the winter, softball in spring. Em's a team player, even when the team is just me and Brian.

Me and Em have fooled around a little bit. But that's over now.

Miranda, now, she's something else. She's so far out of Brian's league, she might as well be on another planet. I mean, she's a lifeguard! Totally in shape, one of the most popular girls in school since kindergarten, stellar grades. Her shiny black hair—let's call it sleek—and high cheekbones make her more like a model and less like a real person.

Any normal guy—like me—would know his place with a girl like Miranda. But Brian . . . I love the guy, but he's not normal. He actually believes he might get a chance to hook up.

Not helping to dispel this illusion? Emily was on the dive team with her. So she knows Brian's name is actually not Toad, which is what most girls call him.

"Anyway, gotta go. Things to do," I say, and sling my leg over my bike.

Brian rolls his eyes at me. "*Things to do?* What, you got a job now?"

We both know the "job" I had last year is gone. The farm barely had a summer stand then, eking out a few bucks selling fresh eggs and sweet corn to the neighbors. But the chickens were eaten last fall (sorry, chickens) and the corn is dead.

I stare at the patch of earth under my bike's front tire. Hard. Dry. Empty. Three long months stretch out before me. Jesus, what do I have to look forward to this summer? Smoking weed and riding dirt bikes with Brian? Watching him make a fool out of himself as he lusts after Miranda? Sounds like a path to loserdom. Like father, like son.

"I could get you a job," Brian says. "Making deliveries," he adds, lowering his voice and glancing furtively around the drive-in.

I know that look. "Dude, I'm not gonna be a weed guy."

"I said you'd make deliveries. Who said anything about dope?"

I sit back on my bike and cross my arms over my chest. Am I that desperate for cash? We've been living on Mom's income for a long time, but how much longer I don't know. Granddad's farm and house are paid off, thank god, but I'm savvy enough about finances to know there are taxes and other crap that have to be paid each month. I often heard Mom and Dad arguing late at night, about how Dad needed to contribute more and take responsibility and *face facts.* That's one of Mom's favorite phrases, as in "Face facts, DJ, this farm can't run itself." Or, "Face facts, Matty, you'll crack your head open if you don't wear a helmet."

I wonder if she's telling herself, *Face facts, Lorna, that jerk is gone and he's not coming back.*

But that's a good thing. Isn't it?

I hear the flick of a lighter and look up to see Brian with

a brand-new joint, a little on the skinny side but it'll do. He doesn't light it himself but hands both the Bic and the joint to me.

"You kinda look like you need it," he says.

I don't hesitate. I fire it up, take two quick tokes, and hold the smoke in my lungs for as long as I can. Finally I give it back and exhale.

"So . . . the lake?" I ask Brian.

My friend shakes his head. "Nah, this is good."

I tilt my face up to the sky and feel the sun warm my cheeks. *Yeah, this is good.*

It doesn't take long for every muscle in my body to turn to jelly and for my head to feel like it's filled with helium, expanding farther and farther out into the Universe. Fleeting bits of memories, of Dad and me, of other summers, pop into my brain.

"Have you ever thought about what's out there, Junior? All the billions and billions of stars in our galaxy?" my dad asked me often when I was a kid. Strictly speaking, I'm not a Junior, since he's David James and I'm David Matthew, but I didn't care. Not then. We'd be sitting outside on a hot summer night, and he'd point up to the sky, index finger tracing the outline of the Big Dipper from the North Star. He'd explain the difference between constellations and asterisms and how Pluto was booted from planet to star and then upgraded back to dwarf planet.

When the willow trees went bare in late fall, we could

see the field from the porch. Mom wouldn't let us spend too much time over there. "If your father could live in that field, he'd do it in a heartbeat, Matty," she'd say with a nervous smile. "Now don't you get caught up in it too."

My father would laugh and wave her away. "He won't, Lorna, he won't." But as soon as she was gone, he'd whisper, "It's a part of our history. The Jones family history. It's special. I'm special. We're special."

Special. My dad was born to be something great, to do something great. He knew that because on the night he was born, a spaceship landed in the field next to his house. It landed at the exact moment of his birth. Coincidence?

No such thing as coincidences. Not where the Universe is concerned.

In 1965, in our rural Pennsylvania town, a spaceship landed, or so locals said. It crashed at two in the morning in the field next to the Jones Family Farm, in one of the cornfields Granddad Jones owned at the time. He didn't see it land but he felt it—the whole town felt it. Some people reported seeing a fireball in the sky just before the ground shook, while others said they felt electricity in the air like nothing they'd ever felt before. Clocks stopped. Watches went dead. Refrigerators and oven doors opened and closed; lights turned on and off.

My grandfather, who wasn't known for his curiosity, nevertheless tossed a blanket over his wife, who'd just given birth to her first son, and ran outside without another word. When he came back an hour later, his face was gray and his clothes were covered in soot. He calmly picked up his wailing newborn, whispered in his ear, and immediately the baby stopped crying. My grandmother never knew what he'd said.

The field burned the rest of the night while firemen from the whole county valiantly fought the blaze. The next morning, as the sun rose over the farm, there was a clamor in the field. Hundreds of Granddad's neighbors surrounded what appeared to be a huge metal cone, dented into the earth like it had been pounded in by a giant hand. At the base of it were etched weird hieroglyphics no one had ever seen before, which isn't saying too much since the town is relatively remote. The local press took photos and interviewed witnesses.

The excitement, said those who were there, was palpable. Finally something to put the small town on the map! Whether you believed it was an alien ship or a piece of a Russian spacecraft, it was remarkable that anything had happened in our town.

That was December 9, 1965.

On December 10, the military arrived and took it all away.

9:28 P.M.

Dinner is quiet. The absence of Dad's voice, as grating as it could be when he was prattling on, makes the farmhouse feel even bigger and emptier. Mom picked up KFC on the way home from work, which helps a little. Grease eases a lot of pain.

Not that we're in pain. Not me, not Mom.

"What'd you do today?" she asks me over wine and Cokes. She's dressed again in her pink pj's, which makes me wonder if she went to work like that and I just didn't notice. But no, my mother is tough, not crazy.

I shrug. "Rescued a cat from a tree. Helped an old lady cross the street. Shit like that."

"Nice."

"How about you?"

"Saved the world from a deadly virus."

"Damn. You got me beat."

My mother waves a drumstick in the air. "Well, it was just one person and he had strep throat, but it *could have been the plague.*"

"Until you stopped it."

"Until I stopped it." She starts to eat the chicken but takes a sip of wine instead. "What's on the agenda for tomorrow? More of the same?"

I cock my head, chewing. "That would be my best guess." Which is true. Maybe we'll go to the lake, or if it's stupid hot, we'll go to the mall at the edge of town and soak up the AC. "And you?"

My mother drops the drumstick and rubs her eyes with her forefinger and thumb like she wants to poke her eyeballs out. "I should probably go see Jack."

My uncle. Carol's husband. Dad's brother. "He doesn't know?"

Mom scowls. "You think he didn't get the memo?" Before I can answer, she lets out a breath. "His note was probably better written than mine. Carol went to Penn State, after all."

And Dad went to the School of Life.

"He might know more about what's going on," she says.

I rip into a hunk of thigh meat, chewing sloppily. "What

do you mean? What else do you need to know?"

Mom rests her hands on the table. "It's not . . . it's not that simple, Matty. When people leave—"

"The ones left behind get on with their lives." How does she not understand this?

She starts to say something, her mouth open and moving, but then she stops and smiles. "You're right. That's what we do. But . . . Jack and I still need to talk." When she sees me about to protest, she quickly adds, "He owns the farm too. He might want to do something with it now that DJ's gone."

"I doubt it. What would he want with a farm? It's dead. And even if it were doing well, he's already got a job."

My uncle's a car salesman. He met Carol about five years ago when she was looking for a car. She didn't buy one but she married Jack. In retrospect, maybe my uncle should have tried harder to sell her on the car instead.

"Matty, I don't want to argue. I'm tired and it's been a long-ass day." My mom slumps forward with her chin on her hands. "Would you mind cleaning up tonight?"

"Oh yeah, sure, sure." I scan the table. I can easily scarf down the rest of the chicken and sides. Except for the green beans. Who likes that crap?

"Thanks. And I can do the coffee in the morning. Sleep all you want," she says, her words a bit slurred. Too much wine, not enough wings? Nah, she's probably just tired.

She leaves, taking her glass with her, and something

occurs to me. "Hey? You called him, right? You called his cell?"

My mother's head bobs and then stops. "Oh. No. I didn't."

"Did you . . . do you want *me* to?"

Her eyes brighten. "Would you?"

I reach for my phone and scroll through my contacts. Is he under "Dad" or "DJ"?

"They have GPS, right?" Mom creeps back to the table. "Like, we could find him through his phone?"

"He's not . . . Mom, he's not *lost*."

My mother's cheeks flush. "I know."

I tap the phone icon next to my dad's number and wait for it to connect. I feel hyperaware of my mom's anxious breath beside me. It rings once, then twice, then . . .

The sound of the *Enterprise*'s transporter, a ghostly shimmer of chimes, echoes in the empty house.

Dad's ringtone. He left his phone here.

My mother's face falls but she recovers quickly. "All right, so . . . I'll let Jack know." She pushes herself away from the table.

"Yeah, sure." What does she *care*? He's gone and it doesn't matter. We don't need him.

As soon as my mother is out of the room, nausea hits me, a thick, gross wave of the meat sweats. I wrap the leftovers quickly and toss them into the fridge for breakfast.

A whine startles me; Ginger's at the screen door. "You

want out, girl?" Her tail swishes from side to side on the floor. I flip the latch and she tears like a bolt toward the field as soon as I open the door. "When you gotta go, you gotta go."

While I wait for her to pee and do a sniff around the yard, I text-harass Brian about Miranda. Ginger usually returns quickly, panting and wagging her tail, ready for a treat before bedtime, but after a few minutes, she's still not back.

I stick my head out into the darkness and glance around. She's not in the side yard doing her business, not in her doghouse waiting for a Milk-Bone.

"Ginger! Ginger! Come on, girl!" I clap my hands and whistle.

Only silence in response.

What the hell . . . Where is she? Seriously, with this dog. I step into the yard, cup my hands around my mouth, and shout her name until I'm hoarse.

Fine, whatever. Let her stay out all night. She'll be back. She'll have to eat.

Out in the empty field, the "space field," something moves, catching my eye. A flash of gold—it has to be my dog. "Ginger? Ginger!" I can just about see the white of her tail flicking in the light of the moon. Damn dog.

The field isn't far—just about fifty yards away—but I have to cross a stream to get there. My dad, in his crappy Pennsylvania accent, calls it a "crick." Water burbles over mossy rocks; a tangle of weeping willow branches drip across the surface. I carefully hop from rock to rock, pushing away the soft branches until I reach the other side.

The field is not empty.

There is my dog. And . . . a girl.

I blink a few times to make sure it's not a trick of the moonlight, but no, Ginger's sitting at the feet of a girl.

According to my dad, people used to travel up and down the coast to check out the space field, *to feel its energy*, he said. But that was years ago. Since I've been alive, maybe a couple dozen or thirty visitors have trooped in and taken pictures.

But no one came in the middle of the night. There is quite literally nothing to see.

This is really weird. A shiver runs down my back even though the air is still and warm.

"Hello!" I call as I approach. "Is my dog bothering you?" I don't want to scare her. Strange guy. Strange dog. Strange night.

She turns to me and her body is in silhouette. Long, slim legs and a slender figure, awkwardly skinny. Her arms dangle by her sides from her shoulders as if they're pinned to a clothesline, and her shoulder-length hair looks white under the light of the moon. Not blond, but stark, flat white.

I raise my hand in a wave, expecting her to lift hers in return, but she just stands there, unmoving. I know she sees me. Whatever. I'm here to get the dog and go home.

"Ginger! Come on, girl! Let's go!"

Ginger, that disloyal canine, stares up at the girl, completely ignoring me.

"Treats, Ginger! Come on! Treat time!" Not even that can tempt her. I wish I had a biscuit with me, or even a chunk of that cold KFC, but I'm empty-handed.

Out of nowhere, a wind kicks up around us, lifting leaves and bits of paper from the ground and whirling them in the air. The breeze feels electrically charged; the hairs on my arms and neck stand up.

What the hell . . .

The girl's arms lift from her sides, as if she were about to take flight, but instead she waves her hands and fingers like the air itself is tangible, touchable. Her long fingers grasp for a leaf, for a candy wrapper, but each twirls out of her reach, teasing her and then escaping.

I hear a twinkle of delight, a thin whisper of a laugh, when her hand finally plucks a leaf from the air. Both hands hold the leaf reverently, as if it were something sacred in her palms, and she brings it closer to her face.

Is she going to eat it? No, that would be crazy. My feet find their way closer to her until I'm just a yard away. I watch, entranced, as she brings the leaf to her nose to sniff it. Suddenly her tongue darts out.

"Don't!" I yell. "My dog probably peed on that."

"My dog probably peed on that." Did I really just say . . . ?

Why yes, yes, I did.

The wind dies down just as quickly as it started, almost as if my shout disturbed something. The girl glances up at me, her eyes narrowing.

"Uh, hi," I say again. Her gaze on me is so intense, boring into me as if she were studying me. I bend down to Ginger's level and pat the dog on her stupid fat head. "Okay, Ginger, let's go." She once again ignores me, but this time I grab hold of her collar and begin to pull her up. "Come on, girl," I urge, but she is sixty pounds of stubborn. "Ginger. Let's. Go."

I feel like an idiot in front of this girl. "Uh, this happens sometimes. She gets in moods, you know?"

There's a long pause before the girl responds. "She's a dog, yes?"

Did I hear that right? Ginger's big, but she's not the size of a horse or a goat or anything. "She's a Lab. A retriever," I clarify when I see the girl tilt her head to one side. "You know, like if I throw a ball or something, she'll fetch it and bring it back to me."

The girl picks up a soft black bag from the ground next to Ginger. I half expect her to take out a tennis ball and test my theory, but instead she pulls out a small notebook wrapped in a thick rubber band. Turning from me and shielding the notebook from my eyes, she jots something with a quick hand.

Does she seriously not know Ginger is a dog? I shake my head to myself. Nah, couldn't be. She probably just doesn't recognize a Labrador retriever. Speaking of . . .

"Come on, Ginger, you lazy piece of . . . Let's go home."
But the dog has planted her haunches into the earth.

"Is this your home?" I hear the girl ask.

"Yeah, over there." I wave a hand toward the weeping
willows and she gasps.

"The tree is your home."

I laugh. "Uh, no. Behind the tree. The house past the
crick—I mean, creek." I gaze beyond the small stream to
my house. The kitchen light is still on, as is the light in my
mother's room.

"You, uh, you live around here?" I ask the girl. I'm pretty
sure I've never seen her, and our town is small. Like, super
small. Everyone knows everyone.

I'm totally not surprised when she shakes her head.
She's a visitor—one of *those* people. Naturally. There's no
way a girl standing in an empty field in rural Pennsylvania
in the middle of the night is going to be normal. Why would
I think otherwise?

She steps around the dog to get a closer look at the
house, and when she glances back at me, I finally see her
in the moonlight. I notice her eyes first, round and wide
and framed by finely arched brows, her cheeks tawny and
unblemished, her chin tapering to a gentle point. Her hair
falls past her shoulders, white over a wispy layer of black.
Her long neck sinks into a sharp collarbone, and she is so
thin I can see the outline of her ribs under her lightweight

T-shirt. Her skirt, cropped midthigh, looks like a child's tutu, layer upon layer in cotton-candy colors: pink and blue and yellow and green, all pale and sparkly as if dusted with starlight.

She is like no girl I've ever seen, certainly no girl from our small town. She looks like she might float away with the leaves if the wind picks up again, and I have a sudden urge to grab hold of her bony wrists and tether her to the earth.

"This place is magical," she says. "You and this dog are very fortunate."

She seems to choose her words carefully, as if she's consulting a dictionary in her mind. Her gaze tilts to one side and that white-black hair hangs from the side of her head in long hanks. A wig? It must be. Who has white hair? My hand wants to reach out and sweep it away from her face. I take a conscious step back from her. "I guess it's okay. It's the only place I've ever lived."

"It's magical," she repeats, adding, "I can feel the energy."

I snort. My dad tweeted crap like that a lot: *The field absorbed the energy of the ship when it crashed. We just don't know what to do with it. #PAspaceship #ibelieve*

Please.

"Yeah, well." I leave it at that. "So where are you from?"

Her eyes lift upward and drop back down to meet mine. She smiles, her lips in a tiny pucker.

"Um . . . up in the mountains? Altoona?"

She bobs her chin toward the sky.

"Farther? New York? Canada?"

This time she lifts *my* chin toward the sky; I feel a tingle as her fingertips touch my skin. I gaze upward at the field of stars scattered around the moon. She's telling me, what? She's from the moon?

Hoo boy. We may have a live one here.

"Okay, well, I gotta get home," I say bluntly, pulling away from her touch. I clap my hands and call for Ginger. Finally, the dog rises off her haunches and follows me. We are at the willows, about to cross the stream, when I stop and turn back.

"You gonna be okay by yourself?" I ask. Maybe I should leave Ginger with her, just in case.

She smiles as if she hasn't a care in the world. "My ride will be here soon." She says it in a singsong. *Tra-la-la*, I can almost hear in her voice.

Well, okay. I wave and hop across the creek.

That was a very bizarre way to end my day. A day that began with Dad leaving and ended with . . . this.

Back in the kitchen, I finish cleaning up, wipe down the counters, and throw out the green bean side dish that congealed while I was outside.

I send Brian a text: *dude, new crazy up at the field.*

He writes: *wtf*

shes kinda hot.

she????

Through the window I try to keep an eye on her. The trees are thick with leaves and hard to see through at a casual glance; you kind of have to know what you're looking for.

It's been a long time, maybe a couple of years, since we've had a UFO tourist. My dad used to envision the field being turned into an attraction, complete with a visitors' center where people could buy souvenirs or get their pictures taken.

"Junior, take a look at this map and tell me what you think," he asked me often, pointing out a mock-up on his computer. "Should the parking lot be across the street or should we use our driveway as an entrance? I think we should sell snacks, don't you? People get thirsty in the summertime, and if there's a long line, they might get hungry too."

We were going to get rich. We were going to get famous. We wouldn't need to be farmers anymore.

But he never got very far because the field doesn't belong to us. The government owns that portion of our farm and, like my mother and me, the Department of Agriculture doesn't care about spaceships and blogs about conspiracy theories.

Oh jeez. Is this girl one of *them*? A conspiracy nut?

Ginger pads over to me at the counter while I stare out the window. She paws at my leg until I realize I haven't given her a treat. I grab a biscuit from the bag and give it to her, and when I glance back up, the girl is gone.

No, not gone. She's there, but she's on the ground.

"What the . . ." Did something happen to her? I run out the door with Ginger at my heels, leaping over the creek and through the willows. "Hey! Hey, are you o—"

I stop. She's on the ground, all right, legs stretched in front of her, feet pointed as if she were standing on her toes. Her eyes are wide open, staring straight up at the sky as if she were drinking it in, drowning in the moon and stars. My heart pounds in my chest and my lungs breathe a sigh of relief.

"You're back," she says. "The magnetism of this place. It's so strong, isn't it?"

I lean my hands on my knees to catch my breath. "No," I say at last. "I thought . . . I thought you'd died."

She smiles. "No. Not yet. I have a lot to do before that happens." She pats the ground beside her. "Why don't you sit down for a minute before you go home again?"

Ginger takes that as an invitation to lick the girl's face and then plops down next to her. Whatever. I sit too, pulling my knees to my chest.

"So, what's your name?" I ask.

Her hand snakes over to her notebook but she doesn't pick it up. "I'm . . . Priya," she says slowly, as if she were settling on the name. "That's what people call me."

"Nice to meet you, Priya." I try to shake her hand, but

it's awkward, what with her lying on the ground and me sitting up. "I'm Matthew. People call me Matty. Are you, uh, getting a ride soon?"

"Soon, yes."

No wristwatch, I see, no cell in her hand like every other person I know, although reception at the field is notoriously bad anyway. A sign, my dad often tweeted, that something alien had landed there (#ibelieve). In reality, probably a sign we need more cell towers in rural Pennsylvania.

Priya reaches a hand to pet Ginger. I notice it trembles and I wonder, is she nervous? Hungry? Mom gets trembly when her blood sugar is low, and she ends up scarfing down one of my father's candy bars.

"You thirsty or anything? Need something to eat?"

"Eat?" Priya shakes her head and continues to stroke the dog's coat. "I don't need to eat."

I laugh. "Everyone needs to eat."

"Not me."

Of course all this talk of eating rouses my dog from her slumber. She nuzzles her nose under Priya's hand, startling her. "Her nose! It's so cold!"

"Well. Yeah. She's a dog."

She stares at her fingertips, eyes wide. "And it's wet."

"Have you *never* petted a dog before?"

"No. But I sensed she wanted me to touch her."

"You *sensed* it?" Kind of hard not to know when Ginger wants to be petted. It's just about all the time. "She likes it when you scratch behind her ears." I show her how to rub behind Ginger's ears and the dog happily thumps her tail against the ground. Priya giggles and reaches her hand toward the dog, but her arm jerks suddenly and instead of touching Ginger's ears, she grabs hold of the dog's wagging tail. Ginger yelps and yanks away as she jumps up.

"Oh!" Priya's eyes fill with tears. "I hurt her."

"Nah, she's okay."

"No, no, I hurt her." She covers her face with her hands and begins to weep. "I'm so sorry. We are instructed specifically to harm no one."

We? What does *that* mean? Ginger is fine, she has to see that. And yet, those tears are absolutely real too.

I pull Priya's hands from her face and hold them. Her long fingers are so cold, like tendrils of ice; I can feel every knuckle of bone in them through delicate skin.

But it's her eyes that hit me like a punch to the gut. They're pools, deep and wide, the water threatening to overspill if she blinks. She's actually—truly—upset.

"It's okay, really, it's fine. Watch." I call Ginger's name, and she trots over to me. I guide Priya's hand behind one of Ginger's ears and let her scratch for a minute or two. The dog instantly sprawls on the ground, wallowing in the attention. Finally, Priya smiles.

"She's not injured. I did not permanently harm her." She stops scratching for a moment and reaches for her notebook. Shielding it from my view again, she scribbles on a page with a pen, then stops, cocks her head to one side, and writes some more. She glances up at me from under her white hair. "Observations," she says, tapping the pen on the book.

Why are the pretty ones always insane? That's a famous quote—from a philosopher, isn't it? Or maybe *The Simpsons*? I glance out at the road beyond the weeping willows, but there isn't a single flicker of light meaning a car is on its way here. I wonder how long she'll give it till she needs to call for a lift.

Which reminds me . . . my home is waiting for me. Mom will flip out if she gets up and I'm gone. Two men disappearing on her in one day would really freak her out—and piss her off. I stand up and brush the dirt from my pants.

But Priya looks so small and fragile. What if something happens to her before her ride comes? I search the field for animals or weirdos, but the place is deserted, as it usually is.

"Look, I have to go. But I'm right over there if you need anything, okay?"

Her smile is placid and calm. "Okay."

"Your cell won't work here—"

"Cell?"

"Cell phone. You have one, right?"

She puts her hand on her bag as if she's checking for one and then shakes her head.

"Well, if you need to make a call or want to use the

bathroom, come on over. I'll leave the side door open." I point again toward the house. She can't miss it; we're the only family on this side of the street for about half a mile.

When I look back at her, her nose is buried in her notebook; a diamond stud sparkles in the moonlight. "So, um, good luck getting home."

When she looks up at me, I stick my hand out. She stares at it, confused, until I take her hand and shake it gently.

I feel like a moron, but a smile lights up her face. She releases my hand and holds hers out to Ginger, who, being a dog that passed obedience school as a puppy, knows "shake."

"Good-bye, Matthew. Good-bye, Ginger."

The dog licks Priya's nose and then joins me as we start down the gentle slope toward the creek for the second time that night—or morning, I guess it is now. I resist the urge to glance back over my shoulder. She'll be fine. She's what, seventeen? Eighteen? Old enough to take care of herself. And I'm pretty sure she was lying about not having a phone. Is there anyone on this planet who doesn't own a cell?

2:11 A.M.

Back at the house, I grab my phone from the kitchen counter and swipe the screen. Brian sent me a dozen messages while I was gone, most involving the word *girl*.

Yo, hot girl? yaaaaasssss

My fingers dance on the screen, but nothing I type feels quite right. How to describe Priya? How to explain the pretty, crazy, pretty-crazy girl who's alone in an empty field and acts like she's never petted a dog before?

Brian's going to ask me what I've been smoking. Without him.

I tap the screen and send a text: *white hair, brown eyes, skinny*

Almost immediately Brian texts me back: *Legs?*

Long

Sweet

I laugh and type an emoji with a middle finger. Repeat, repeat, repeat.

The clock on the stove says it's way late. I gotta sleep. It's the farmer in me.

Dude?

Tomorrow

Lake with Em?

Do I want to go with Brian and Emily to the lake? With Brian? Yes. With Em?

I type a question. Shake it to undo. Type it again. Shake it again.

Does Em have to go?

I feel my pulse throb in my ears while I wait for Brian's response. I get a soda, suck it down, crush the can under my sneaker, and give Ginger another treat—all in the time it takes Brian to answer me:

Yeah. She's driving.

I scowl at my phone. Just as I'm about to type "no," another text comes from my best friend:

Going to gran's for a week, btw

When?

Day aft tmrw.

A week away will help. Well, it'll help me, at least. I bang out "yes" and hit send. And now it's really time for bed. As

I stumble past the door, I unlock it, just in case Priya needs to come in and pee or whatever. I also leave my phone on the counter. If she really doesn't have a cell, she might need to borrow one.

I take one last look out the window, searching for her through the tangle of willow branches. Yep. Still there, sitting on the ground, leaning back on her hands, and staring deep into the sky. The moon silhouettes her tutu and white hair.

What a crazy, crazy girl.

DAY TWO

9:09 A.M.

A rustle in my room wakes me. Mom is rummaging in my closet.

"Hey . . . ? Whatcha looking for?"

When she glances over her shoulder, I catch a glimpse of red-rimmed eyes. Has she been crying? *Please don't tell me she's crying over that asshole.* I mush the pillow behind my head into a ball and punch it lazily with my fist.

She clears her throat. "Your father had a lockbox with important papers. Yay big?" She holds her hands about ten inches apart.

I know it. I nod. "So?"

"So. It's got the deed to the farm from your grandfather. I need it for Uncle Jack."

I pull the covers over my head, but it's already hot up here. The stone farmhouse stays cool in the summer, but not on the second floor. I feel my mother's finger poke my shoulder through the sheet.

"Well? Thoughts?" She paces my room, absently stepping over my crap spread across the floor. She doesn't seem to notice any of it.

"Did you check the shop?" I yawn and allow myself to tumble off the bed and onto a soft pile of jeans and T-shirts. My mother kicks me with her bare feet.

"Quit it. Aren't you supposed to be at work?" I ask.

She's half dressed, wearing the bottoms of her nurse's scrubs with her pajama top. She's not even embarrassed about it. "My shift doesn't start till ten." She kicks her way through my crap as she leaves my room. I really don't want to get up, but I feel compelled to follow her to the guest room, the one where Grandmom Jones gave birth to her two sons. I'm too sleepy to shudder at the visual like I usually do. Mom opens drawers and closets that haven't seen daylight in years. Why she thinks Dad would put anything of value here is beyond me.

"The shop, Mom. Have you checked the shop yet?" I ask again.

She brushes past me as she stalks the top floor of the house, from my bathroom to hers, from the linen closet to the hamper (the hamper? Seriously?). I stop for a long-ass pee, and by the time I finish, I find her in her bedroom, sitting on the edge of the queen-size bed that is rumpled on one side only. She stares at the floor.

"Mom. Mom," I say, until she finally looks up. Her fingertips hold her chin.

"What."

"Did. You. Check. The. Shop?"

She sighs and glances around the room, her eyes darting from corner to corner. I can almost read her thoughts: *Is it in the closet? Under the bed? Between the layers of winter clothes?* And then we both hear a squirrel scamper across the roof and my mother's gaze lingers on the ceiling. *Maybe it's in the attic?*

"The place you should look is the shop. If it's going to be anywhere, it's going to be there."

She shakes her head and slides off the mattress, hastily starting to make the bed behind her. "I don't have time. Will you?"

"Me?"

"What, you have something better to do? A job you're rushing off to, maybe?"

Uh, what the hell? I think but don't say, and then I realize why she didn't go to the shop to look for my dad's lockbox:

If it's not there, it means he really is gone. Gone and not coming back.

"Yeah, I'll do it. Whatever." I don't care if it's not there. I hope it won't be. That would be the final nail in the coffin of hope she's holding. It would at last blow out the torch she's carrying. It would. . . oh god, coffee.

"It's only been one day, Matty."

"Sure. One day. With Carol, Mom. He left with Carol. You got the note and . . ." She's making the bed with furious gestures, shoving the pillows under the sheets and fiercely smoothing out the wrinkles on her side of the bed. Clearly not in the mood to hear logic. "Whatever."

I stagger down the back staircase and go through the motions: water, filter, Maxwell House. While I wait for the coffee to brew, I go to text Brian but my phone isn't where I left it. Rubbing my eyes, searching the kitchen, thinking maybe it slid under something, a flyer for dry cleaning or an old grocery list, but it isn't anywhere.

"Mom! Mom!" I shout up the back stairs. "Did you move my phone?"

"Your what?"

"My phone! Did you see it when you came down this morning?"

"Your phone? No."

"Are you—"

"I have to get dressed, sweetie." A second later, I hear the water running in her bathroom.

I know I put it on the counter last night after I said good-bye to Priya.

Priya. I think of her and my memory is . . . hazy. But she *was* real, wasn't she?

I run to the side door, the one I left unlocked, and my heart thumps hard in my chest. In the daylight, the field looks even more forlorn and empty.

Empty. It's . . . empty. Priya is gone.

And so, evidently, is my cell. Did she take it? Or just borrow it to call her boyfriend for a ride?

Why "boyfriend," Matty? Could have been just a friend.

It wasn't the best phone, wasn't the newest "i-" anything, but it was mine and it had a pretty decent data plan.

Back in the kitchen, the smell of fresh coffee fills the air and I breathe in a bit of caffeine high.

Well, I guess she wasn't lying about not having a phone before.

"And she has one now," I say to Mr. Coffee. "You're welcome, Priya."

Ginger paws the door just then, and I realize I haven't taken her for a walk yet. Crap. I'll give her breakfast first. "Do you remember that crazy girl last night, Ginger? Do you?" I ask as I let her inside and grab the kibble. "Do you remember that beautiful yet crazy girl?"

"What beautiful crazy girl?" I hear my mother ask. She rushes in, fully dressed now, her hair gelled and spiked properly, looking way more professional than she did a few minutes ago. She hustles about, gathering her things for the day. She snaps her fingers a couple of times and points to a shelf high above her. "Grab me a travel mug from up there, okay?"

Even with her orthopedic shoes on, my mother is puny compared to me and my father. When things were good with Dad, he and I would tease her about being so tiny, playing keep-away with her cell or throwing her between us like she was a doll. Ginger would bark and jump too. Usually, things weren't that good.

"You want the silver one?" I take it down from a cupboard above the stove.

"What beautiful crazy girl?" she asks again.

"'Why yes, the silver one goes perfectly with my gray hair,'" I say.

"I do not have gray hair. What girl, Matty?"

I deftly sub the mug for the coffeepot so it can drip directly into it. *Clever me.* "No one. I was talking to the dog."

"You're not sneaking out at night to hang out with some girl, are you?"

"No. Mom. Stop. No girls, no sneaking. Just . . . take your coffee, okay?"

I hand her the mug without looking at her. "Where's your phone?" I ask. I dig through her canvas bag and find not just her phone but my dad's as well. Why the hell hasn't she crushed that thing already?

Whatever. I dial my number and hope Priya answers,

even if she's a million miles away by now.

I take the phone outside so Mom won't interrogate me, practicing what I'll say when Priya picks up.

You took my phone, you wacko! Or maybe, *Can I pretty please have my phone back?* Or—

Wanna hang out sometime?

No, no, no. *Hellllll* no. I stop thinking with my pants. I'm going with the first choice.

My palms start to sweat as the phone rings once, then twice, and a third time. On the other end, the screen should be reading "Lorna" since I have no desire to have "Mom" come up on my caller ID at any point in time.

I hear my own voice in my ear: *"It's Matty. Text me. I don't do fucking voice mail."*

Why didn't she pick up? I dial again. A minute later, I hear my message again and cringe. Crap, I've got a super-annoying voice.

Out of the corner of my eye, I see my mother at the kitchen door, hands on hips, watching me. I head straight toward the creek and the willows.

My phone, wherever it is, rings a second and third time.

"Answer it, Priya!"

I stand in the center of the completely empty field. No Priya, no notebook, no black bag, not even an impression in the dry earth of where she and I sat and looked up at the stars. Maybe she was never here at all.

But my phone is still missing.

When I hear my voice mail for the third time, I leave a message. "Hey, Priya, it's Matty. You have my phone. Could you bring it back, please? Or, like, send it to me or something? Thanks."

I have a sinking feeling I'll never see that phone again. A car honks; Mom is backing her Honda out of the driveway. As I approach, she holds her hand out to me. "Can I have that?"

Reluctantly I give her cell back to her.

"You lose yours?"

"Something like that."

She shrugs. "Sucks to be you." She's just pissed she hasn't found Dad's lockbox. Still, who needs her crap? It's not like it's *my* fault. "What are you doing today?"

"*Not* calling or texting anyone."

"Ha-ha, funny boy. There's a thing called a landline."

I make a face. "If you're a hundred years old."

She holds up her middle finger and I match it with mine, touching our knuckles together like we're a profane version of the Wonder Twins. "Go. Clean the house."

"Go. Heal the sick." I feel Ginger's tail swish against the backs of my legs and wonder how she got outside. Mom must have let her out. "What are we doing today, girl? Cleaning? Nah, I didn't think so."

Summer is not about cleaning the house or chasing

after your stupid father. It's about hanging out at the lake and riding dirt bikes and maybe smoking a little weed to make those two things even more enjoyable.

But I can't stop thinking about the imaginary girl who has really stolen my cell phone.

11:13 A.M.

When we were little kids, Brian and Emily and I thought the underground passageway that connects the basement to my dad's workshop was the coolest thing ever. If it was raining or snowing, we could actually walk underneath the earth from the house to the shop. Dad kept a potbellied stove burning on the coldest days, and he'd let us hang out with him if we swept up the ashes and brought in the firewood.

I wasn't ever supposed to go in there when he wasn't around, which of course I did. How else was I going to learn about girls and sex? Dad never cleared the cache in his computer, so I could look at all the porn he looked at.

I also learned about the Universe. Dad and I had our own telescopes so we could look at the stars side by side. On his walls were celestial maps and charts, miraculous photos from the Hubble, and a poster signed by Ray Bradbury. The shop was a mini observatory, a weird combination of Hollywood and NASA. For all of my father's interest in the sky and aliens, he still had a fanboy's obsession. It wasn't enough for *him* to believe a ship had landed in the field next to his house. He needed everyone else to believe it too.

And I did. For a long time, I believed.

Leaving the basement through the secret passageway makes me feel like I'm nine again, giggling with Brian and Em as we sneak underground. I'm about two feet taller now, though, so I have to bend over at the waist to avoid hitting my head on the ceiling of the tunnel. It's dark in here but I know every step, every inch of the way. When I get to the halfway point between shop and house, I stop and place my hands on the stone ceiling, pressing upward. We used to pretend we could hold the Earth high above our heads; we were superheroes of the underworld.

It could have been a claustrophobic feeling in that tunnel, the thought of tons of dirt on top of us, but it wasn't. It made me feel safe and secure, although maybe it was having my best friends with me that made me feel that way.

The shop itself is just a small shed with a concrete floor and stone walls, and it's partially built into a mound of earth in the side yard. From the outside it kind of looks like a hobbit's home, but I seriously doubt Granddad used Tolkien as his architectural inspiration. More likely, it helped the insulation, keeping it cool in the summer and warm in the winter.

I involuntarily shudder when I step into the shop. It's chilly here, yes, but it's also like stepping back in time. So much of what I remember from my childhood is still here: the posters, the maps, the charts, the stove. But something is missing.

The telescope. There's only one—mine.

Dad must have taken his with him.

As much as I didn't believe his bullshit anymore, as much as I wanted him to be a regular dad I could count on . . . there's something really sad about seeing my telescope sitting by itself next to the woodstove.

It looks . . . lonely.

Something sinks into my stomach then, and I feel my muscles tighten around it, squeeze it, crush it. I have to be glad he's gone. I have to believe it will be better for Mom. For both of us. For everyone.

A chart on the wall catches my eye, one of the few he left behind. It's a map of potentially habitable planets in what's called the Goldilocks Zone. An exoplanet has to be in *just* the right place in order for life—as *we* know it—to form there. A dwarf planet like Pluto, for instance, is too far away from our sun to support life. It's an icy rock with a surface temperature of minus 387 degrees Fahrenheit.

Still other planetoids, like our moon, are tidal-locked, so one hemisphere is always facing the object it's connected to gravitationally. With our moon, that means one half of it never sees the Earth. That's the dark side of the moon.

Aaaannnd . . . how do I still know all this?

Why did it stick in my brain?

I don't want it there, not any more than I want phone numbers of friends who moved away in my cell phone. Makes me wish I could stick a jump drive into my ear and suck out all the useless information. Maybe then I'd have room for English lit.

I stare at the chart, where Gliese 581c and Kepler-69c are crossed out. Both were once considered options for habitability, but no longer. At least not according to who-ever designed this chart.

I run my finger along the poster, tapping each of the exoplanets in turn. Every one of them is classified accord-ing to how Earth-like it is as well as how far from us it is. Some of the exoplanets that scientists consider the most likely to be habitable are hundreds of billions of miles away. Those *Star Trek* crews would have to boldly go pretty damn far to find anything or anyone remotely like us.

Unless, of course, *they* come to *us*.

Which is exactly what my father and all his wack-job friends believe happened.

Online, DJ Jones is a minor crazy among an entire internet *filled* with crazies—legions of UFO chasers and self-professed alien abductees who DJ wrote to and chatted with every day. Like him, they believe we're not alone in this universe.

When I was a kid, I loved learning about the stars and the Milky Way. I loved watching Captains Kirk and Picard and Janeway whoosh from quadrant to quadrant on the *Enterprise*, and I loved reading *The Martian Chronicles*.

It was science. It was real. And what was fiction was *science* fiction.

But Dad went beyond that at some point.

When Mom and I weren't looking, he began to engage in conspiracy theories online. He egged his fans on, and they followed him from Twitter to his own blog. He was the Boy Who Was Born Next to a Spaceship Landing. He was Special. He was Blessed by Aliens.

It seemed like, in the blink of an eye, Dad became self-centered and egotistical. He never thought about me or Mom or Uncle Jack anymore. And what kind of a person prefers talking crap online with strangers to working and raising a family? What kind of a person takes off with his brother's wife?

The kind that we're better off without (#ibelieve).

Good riddance.

But something else feels weird in this workshop. Something I can't quite put my finger on. Maybe something is out of place. My telescope, maybe? It looks clean, the layers of dust wiped from the tripod and tube. My dad must have done that, hoping I'd come back someday.

I continue to poke around until I give up. I'm not sure what's bothering me about the place. I take one last glance around the workshop and snap off the light.

No lockbox.

I'm done.

It's done.

2:45 P.M.

The lake at noon is crowded with kids and moms, but if we wait until they all go home for their naps, we get the place to ourselves. Unfortunately for my buddy Brian, Miranda the hot lifeguard isn't working today.

"Why, dude?" he whines as soon as we settle our towels on the sand. "I was all set to drown today."

"You're an idiot. What if she isn't watching and you actually do drown?" his sister asks. "Or her partner rescues you instead?"

I purse my lips and make kissing noises at Brian. "Sure, you could be getting mouth-to-mouth from Eric Miller."

"That wouldn't be so bad," Emily says, not quite under

her breath. She isn't in her old dive team uniform of a navy blue one-piece but instead wears a bikini in pink and red flowers that stands out sharply against the white towel. She unknots her hair and lets it splay behind her. She looks like a painting.

"What's that, Em? Do you *like* Eric? Do you like, *like* him?" Brian teases.

I avoid looking at her face. I don't want to know if she *likes* Eric Miller.

Fortunately for me, she slips a pair of sunglasses on, shutting out both of us. "Fuck off and drown, Toad."

"Ooh, ouch!" I say.

"Aw, she's gonna miss us when she's at college." Brian grins loopily; he smoked half a joint on our way to the lake. "Dude, tell me about the girl. What's her name?"

I hesitate. "Priya."

"Why didn't you bring her?"

"She went home, that's why."

"You got her digits?"

I instantly think of my phone, which is probably in her bag at this very moment. Oh man, that thing had a brand-new case on it. "Yeah, sort of."

"So text her."

"Not that simple."

"What, she's got a boyfriend?"

I shake my head and laugh. "That would be easy."

"Then what is it?"

"She's . . ."

I don't know where she is and if she's ever coming back and I don't even know why I'm still thinking about her.

I stare down at my feet. I'm wearing sneakers and socks; the sand is scorching and making me sweat. I heel away my Nikes and gym socks before I strip off my T-shirt. "I'm hot like your mother, dude. I gotta get wet."

I do a shallow dive into the lake and come up for air a few feet away. There are two wooden floats off the shore, both empty—I swim for the farthest and pull myself up onto it. With my feet dangling over the side, I'm surely bait for the monsters that live under the surface.

The lake water is cool, the sun toasty, but the breeze makes all the difference in the world. It whisks away the moisture on my skin, like toxins released from my body to rise into the atmosphere. The smells of suntan lotion and sugary melted Popsicles waft toward me from the shore. They are the scents of summer, what defines a hot day in this town.

When I lay my hand flat on the wooden float, I'm reminded of last night, of lying by Priya's side and staring into the sky. Maybe I shouldn't have left her. Maybe I should have waited with her till she was picked up. Maybe I should have asked her where she was from, where she was *really* going.

At the very least, I'd still have my phone.

A couple of minutes later, the float bobs as another swimmer pulls himself up.

Or herself. Emily. Of course. "'Sup."

"Nada mucho."

"So, you met a strange girl in the middle of the night."

I prop myself on my elbows and look at her. Her hair is slicked back from the swim; water drips down her temples and cheeks and lips.

The last time I was alone with Em was a week ago, when we hooked up at a post-grad party.

Afterward, she was all "Matty, we can't do this again. I'm going to college and I don't want a boyfriend," and I was all "No worries, no girlfriend for me, thankyouverymuch," and it was cool.

Except . . . it wasn't cool.

It wasn't . . . enough. For me, it wasn't enough. I kissed her because I felt things for her. I thought she felt the same way. About me. About us. I thought there *could be* an us. I mean, we've known each other forever. But when I asked her out—in person, not on the phone, not in a text—she was all "Get bent, Jones."

Maybe not those exact words, but it *felt* like that.

It *felt* like she said, *Get lost, screw you, why won't you die and let me be.*

And now.

Here she is.

And she's wearing a bikini and she has that face that I've kissed before and that body that I've wrapped my arms around and I . . .

"Who is she?"

I blink. "Huh? Priya?"

"Is that her name? That's . . . different." Em's on the other side of the float with her knees pulled up, one leg crossed over the other as if she were sitting on the couch at home. She's so comfortable in the water, around the water, above the water. Swimming is as natural to her as firing up a bong is to her brother.

"Well, yeah, that's what she said."

"You don't believe her?"

I almost snort a laugh. "Uh, yeah, well, she was . . . kind of crazy."

Emily tilts her head back and looks at me. "Crazy how?"

I wave a hand. "Never mind. She just . . . she was pretty and I guess she was smart."

"You like smart girls."

Our eyes meet for a split second and then she glances away. *That was weird.*

"She had white hair."

"Girls can have white hair."

"Yeah, if they're in a comic book."

"So she's Storm?"

I laugh. "She was *not* Storm. I'm sure it was a wig."

"Girl with a wig. Okay."

"Whatever, Em. Just—"

"She was hot, huh?"

"Can we not talk about this?"

"Why not? You didn't think she was hot?"

"She was, but—"

"We're friends, Matty. I want to know."

Was that my heart that just slammed shut like a prison door? "Right. *Friends*."

Emily combs her fingers through her hair. Water drips off the ends like icicles melting in the sun. "Are we ever going to talk about it?"

"About what? About us being *awesome friends*?"

"Matty . . . you asked me out."

"After we hooked up. Yes, I did. And you—"

Ripped my heart out.

"—said no."

"But it's not because I don't like you."

"Yes, you mentioned that." Is it childish of me to want to stick my fingers in my ears and sing *la la la* to drown out this torturous little chat? Wait, I know. I'll just look out over the lake, watch the water-skiers and the kayakers. *How lovely.*

"And I had a fantastic time with you on grad night."

I hear a *but* coming. Straight at me. I brace myself for the barrage of reasons she is killing my soul.

"Matty, will you just look at me?"

I do, and oddly enough, any urge to press my lips to hers

vanishes into this humid air.

"I like you a lot. And I think you're a really cool guy. But I'm going to college in a couple of months and there's just no future, you know? I can't be your girlfriend."

I spit out, "Who said I—"

"You want a girlfriend. And that's cool but I . . . I don't know. It's just not something I want right now."

My head starts to burn like it's been in the sun for too long, and I guess it has. We've been out here on this float for a hundred years broiling in the heat. I don't want to talk to Emily about this anymore. I don't want to hear her say this crap ever again. It didn't need to be said. I already knew it.

"Right. Okay. Well, thanks for that, uh, clarification." I roll my eyes, which pretty much always pisses her off.

The evil part of me smiles when I see her grit her teeth in response. "You are so childish, Matty. God. Grow up."

"Grow up?" I scoop some water from the lake and splash it on her face. She doesn't even flinch. "Is that grown up?"

She doesn't take the bait, and my imprisoned heart trembles. Maybe I am childish. So what? "We're friends, Em. I get it. We're just friends."

The saving grace to all of this? She and Brian will be gone for a week starting tomorrow.

Back on the shore Brian's waving his arms over his head to get our attention. He's probably bored without us. "I'm going back, all right?"

"Yeah, sure."

She looks confused by my reply, like maybe she didn't really want to blow a hole through my heart. Or maybe I'm just projecting. I glance sideways at her and make her an offer I know she can't refuse. "You wanna race?"

Em perks up and her eyebrows arch. "Race you?"

"Yeah." I kick my feet in the water, making a big splash. "Afraid I'll win?"

"Oh my god, no. I just don't want to embarrass you in front of Brian."

"Bullshit. You'd love to embarrass me in front of Brian."

A smile creeps across her face. "Yeah, I would."

I crouch over the side. Emily takes her sweet time. I can feel the heat of her body next to mine as she bends down, ready to dive in. I have to harden my heart to her. I have to or else I will die a little more every day that we're together. I push Em away and dive into the water, giving myself a head start.

"Cheater!"

A couple of minutes later I haul my butt out of the water—only to find Emily already lying on her towel, face to the sun.

Brian slow-claps. "Congrats, dude, you came in second."

8:56 P.M.

It's kind of cool not having a phone. Mom can't contact me. No one can text me. I don't have to stare at an empty screen and see no calls from Dad. And the thought of Priya holding it, using it, swiping a long, delicate finger across the screen as she plays Angry Birds, which is the only game I have on my phone—it sort of pisses me off but it sort of doesn't.

When Em and Brian drop me at home, after saying good-bye for a week, I see a car in my dad's spot in the garage. For a moment, I freeze; then I realize it's my uncle Jack's. A brand-new Mustang as befits a Ford salesman. He and Mom are inside, sitting at the kitchen table with glasses of wine in front of them. I watch from outside for a few minutes, wondering what they're saying, how much of that bottle they've already had.

Although Jack is ten years younger than my dad, he looks like he's the older brother. Maybe because he has a real job in the real world with real responsibilities. And maybe because he wears a tie and a sad smile. My dad was always in jeans and a T-shirt and sneakers; he looked like an aging but happy-go-lucky skater boy. Tony Hawk, if he hadn't been successful at anything.

Jack leans back in a chair at the table, his long legs stretched in front of him. His tie's gone and his shirt is open at the neck so you can see his undershirt. Yeah, he's a guy who wears undershirts. He also shaves on the weekends and wears his hair in a crew cut in the summer. Like my dad, he isn't a bad-looking dude, but his wrinkles make him look tired.

And now that his wife is gone with his brother—

Ginger barks, startling me and my mom and uncle. They wave me in but I'm not sure I'm ready. The air is gonna be heavy in there. I point at Ginger and raise my voice through the glass. "Gotta take her for a walk."

They don't care. Of course not. They've got wine to drink.

When I get to the side yard, I feel a pull in my gut. I have to look up at the field. I know she's gone but—

She's there.

No. Way.

My stomach flips like a pancake and my heart pounds. I speed-walk to the creek—and jump over it in a single bound like goddamn Superman. And as I'm panting up the short hill, I keep telling myself *this is for my phone*. It's the *phone* I want, not Priya.

She's sitting on the ground, just like the last time I saw her, with her face tilted up to the moon, as if she were bathing in its glow, getting a moontan. Her eyes find me, but she remains motionless and still. "I know you, don't I?"

"Uh, yeah. We met last night." I point at the ground. "Right here."

She smiles serenely. "I sensed that."

"You, uh, you borrowed my phone?" I feel awkward and way too tall standing over her like this, so I crouch down beside her. She looks exactly the same as last night: same top, same tutu skirt, same nose piercing. A silver chain falls over her throat, sparkling in the moonlight. The charm is a droplet of white-black pearl that matches the color of her hair. Would it be too weird to touch it? To lift it from her neck and roll it between my fingers? To feel the smooth surface of the jewel against my skin?

Yes. That would be weird. Hands. To. Self.

"My phone," I say again, strong and insistent. "You took it and I'd like it back."

"Your . . ."

"Phone, my phone."

Her brow furrows; tiny little ridges appear on her

forehead. "No." She elongates the single syllable into three. *No-o-o.*

I glance over at her black bag, which she clutches like it's a part of her. I start to reach for it and she pulls it closer. I drop my knees to the ground and lean over her, inches from her chest and stomach. "Priya, I need my phone back. I only *loaned* it to you."

She sits up, her face so close to mine that I can smell the flowery perfume of her shampoo. Her lips look like pale pink pillows and I notice for the first time that her face is all wide eyes and plump mouth, curves that are at odds with her skinny frame.

"I did not require the use of your phone," she says in a low voice, very formally. "Although I appreciated your offer." She reaches into her bag and takes my phone out with all the flourish of a magician's assistant. When I take it from her, our fingers touch, sparking a wild sliver of electricity that I can feel all the way down to my toes.

No, no, that's the cell phone. Or the dry grass of the field creating a static burst. It's not anything romantic or magic or . . . crazy.

I shake it off. "Well, if you didn't call anyone, then how did you get home?"

She frowns as if I'm stupid. "I'm not home."

"Not now. But you were." I settle back, putting distance between us. "You were gone this morning. Because you went home, right?"

Again, she shakes her head.

"Did your boyfriend come pick you up?"

"Boyfriend?" She twists the word around in her mouth.

I feel my cheeks warm. Did I really just ask her that? "Or girlfriend. Or just friend. Or . . . whatever." I clear my throat and begin again. "You went somewhere today. Where did you go?"

She points to my house.

"No, no. I mean, where did you hang out today if you weren't here or at home?"

Her finger hovers in the air, still aimed at my house.

"Wait, my house? But how . . ." I left the door open for her so she could use the bathroom and my phone, but . . . "Wait," I say again, because I can't quite wrap my mind around what she's implying. "You were in my house? *All day?* But . . . I was there!"

"I saw all the rooms. There were many, many rooms, many places to gather data and then . . ." She wiggles her finger in the air, drawing a path from one place to another. ". . . there."

"The workshop? You were in my dad's workshop?"

She nods. "Yes. Much cooler."

I stare at her and then—I can't help it—I laugh my ass off. The idea that she was *in my house* while I was there and didn't even know it floors me.

"You're so sneaky!"

"Sneaky?"

"Yeah, stealthy. Like a ninja or something." I shake my head. "You're lucky my mom didn't see you. She might have called the cops."

"I would like to meet your mother."

My mind snaps a picture of mom and Jack at the dinner table, drinking and whining about their loser spouses. "Under normal circumstances, yeah, but now? Maybe another time."

Priya's smile is fleeting and wistful. "There will not be another time. I'm going home. Tonight."

"You said you were going home last night."

"Yes. My calculations were imprecise."

"Um . . . okay. So . . . where exactly is your home?"

She raises a long arm toward the sky. I feel a laugh bubble up in my chest. She can't be serious.

"You're from . . . space?"

"A planet near Gliese 581c. It's twenty light-years from Earth."

Ding-ding-ding-ding! Crazy alert. This is not a drill.

"Only twenty, eh? Well, hello, neighbor." If she catches my sarcasm, she doesn't react, which makes me feel kind of bad. I don't want to make fun of her, but these people, the fanatical ones my dad talked to all the time, make it too easy for me to mock them. Aliens? Spaceships? Special magnetic energy? Please. It's all too ridiculous.

"Gliese 581c, you said?"

"Near Gliese 581c."

"Oh, I see. *Near.* That's totally different. Does it have a name that I can pronounce or is it just a bunch of numbers and letters?"

She turns her face toward me and I see in her eyes that she did catch the snark I was throwing. My face flushes with embarrassment.

"It's okay that you don't believe me."

"Kind of an unusual thing to say."

"I think your father would believe me."

I almost choke on my spit. "Excuse me?"

"Your father . . . he's a crazy person too."

Oh no. She must be part of one of my dad's online conspiracy groups. "How do you know my father?"

"I don't."

"Then how—"

"You were thinking he was a crazy person. Like me," she adds.

"That's not true. Not exactly." Actually I don't think my dad is crazy, just that he supports the crazies. Encourages them to believe in conspiracy theories like the government secretly housing aliens in Area 51. But I don't tell Priya this because . . . I have a twisty gut feeling she's one of the crazies.

On the other hand, if she *is* one, maybe she knows where he is. "Priya, do *you*—"

"If you don't know, then I don't know."

"Huh?" I didn't actually finish my sentence. Did I?

Priya falls onto her back and then rolls over to one side, curling herself around Ginger, who fits her big head into the space between Priya's ribs and hips. I have two sets of inquisitive brown eyes looking at me.

"Back on my home planet, we can sense what others are thinking. Not specific thoughts," she says carefully, almost delicately selecting her words. "But on your planet, it's different. It's not sensing but hearing."

"You can hear my thoughts." I roll my eyes. "You're an alien from another solar system and one who can read minds."

She smiles slyly in the moonlight. "How do you know Gliese 581c is in another solar system?"

I sigh. I have to tread lightly with these people. "My father was into astronomy. He might have taught me a few things." *More than a few.*

"How much more?"

I glance at her and she smiles again. "A lot. But it doesn't matter. I'm sorry, but I don't believe you're an alien."

"Why? Don't you believe there's life on other planets?"

I lift my chin and glance up at the sky, spot the North Star. "You know, I should be smoking a joint if we're going to have this discussion."

"A joint?"

Maybe she *is* from another planet. "Never mind."

I lie flat on my back and we both look up into the stars.

My dad and I used to do this when I was young. He'd

sneak me out while Mom was sleeping and we'd count the stars till the sun began to rise. I don't think my father enjoyed being awake during the daylight hours. There was too much pressure, too many responsibilities. At night, we had the vast Universe to contemplate, to discuss, to imagine. We were Captain Kirk and Mr. Spock speeding through the galaxy on missions to explore new worlds and new species. We were Galileo and Copernicus marveling over the planets, Carl Sagan and Stephen Hawking projecting life onto those planets.

I used to feel so connected to my father back then, proud to be his son, thrilled to share his passions. But . . . something changed, something was lost. The magic of the stars dissolved like dust.

I push myself up to a sitting position and lean my face into Priya's. "Who are you?"

"I'm Priya."

"Where are you from?"

"A planet near Gliese 581c, twenty light-years—"

"Where are you really from?"

"I just told you—"

"That's crap and you know it."

She rolls her head from side to side. "No, Matthew, it's—"

"How did you get here?"

"My people were left here for data collection."

"No, how did you *travel* here?"

"We came on a spaceship, through a wormhole."

"If you're an alien life-form, why do you look exactly like a human?"

"Our planet is a lot like this one."

"You speak English there?"

"I speak whatever you speak."

I open my mouth to ask another question, but she sits up and stops me, getting right in my face so that we are nearly nose to nose. "Matthew, my planet is a lot like Earth but much smaller. It has less gravitational force, so we are smaller than humans, lighter than you. We communicate in different ways, through a shared energy field. Our planet is rapidly changing. It's been cooling very quickly, and we've had to adapt and work together to figure out ways to save it. Because of that, we pushed our technology further than yours, which is why we can travel across the universe and you can't. Yet."

She winds her arms around her knees and rests her head on them, weary and exhausted from standing up to me. "Does that answer all the questions in your head?"

Prove it to me, I think. *Take me with you.*

"You can't come with me."

I scowl and look away. I don't believe she can read my mind—that was obviously a lucky guess—but whatever is happening, I'd appreciate it if she stopped doing it. "Why are you here?"

"I told you. Data collection."

I bob my head at her black bag. "That your data in there?"

"Oh no. This couldn't possibly hold everything." She taps her temple with her forefinger. "The data is stored up here."

Oh lord. I laugh and shake my head. She frowns. "Not laughing at you. Just . . . go on."

"It functions like your cloud computing. Everything I have observed here will be incorporated into our world back home. If it's useful to us, it will become part of our culture, our shared education."

"So, you're stealing from us?"

She stares at me for a while, as if she were studying my lips and mouth. My brain? "Not stealing. Borrowing."

A smile escapes me. "Priya, you may not be from Pennsylvania. Hell, you may not be from America at all. You could be . . . I don't know . . ." I shrug.

"I could be what?"

"Indian? Pakistani? It's not like I see a lot of different kinds of people in this Podunk town. My best friend, Brian? His last name is Aoki. My mom said his family caused a huge stir years ago when they moved here. We aren't exactly a cosmopolitan neighborhood."

Priya regards me for a moment. "You speak. Too much."

I can't help but laugh. I let my eyes wander from Priya's white hair and sharp cheekbones past the ridge of her lips and her chin. Her mouth opens and she smiles mischievously, a hint of something sly in her gaze. Her eyes meet mine and slowly-slowly-slowly *blink*, lashes moving through liquid quicksand, swallowing me up. I feel my pulse quicken when she looks at me like that. "What I'm saying is, I believe you're . . . you're not from around here."

"Thank you."

Suddenly her hand flies to her temple. It's as if she'd been struck. She blinks quickly a few times and her brow wrinkles.

"Are you okay?"

"I . . . have . . . pain. . . ." She presses her palm against her forehead, splaying her fingertips. "It's . . . it's . . ." Her eyes dart from side to side as if she's searching for the word.

"Headache? You have a headache?"

She nods. "Yes, yes, that's it."

"Maybe you have some medicine in your bag."

"No. We are forbidden to carry our own remedies." She presses a second palm to her head, gripping it like a vise. She looks like she's in excruciating pain.

I glance over my shoulder at the house. "Come inside. We have aspirin. And Tylenol." I hold my hand out to Priya, but she stares at it quizzically, her eyes registering confusion. When I grab her hand and tug her to standing, she nearly collapses onto me. I catch her and steady her on her feet. Her lips briefly touch my neck and her white hair tickles my mouth before I can set her right.

She holds my shoulders, keeping herself balanced, but

I can see she's faint; her lips tremble and her eyes spin. Should I carry her to the house? Will Mom and Jack freak out?

"My mother's a nurse," I tell her. "She can help you."

Despite her pain, Priya manages to shake her head back and forth. "No," she says brusquely. "That would not be wise."

"But she knows stuff about—"

"No!"

"Okay, okay." I gently lower her to the ground. "But you need something for your headache. Can you use one of . . ." I sigh. I can't believe I'm about to say this. "One of *our* remedies?"

She bobs her head in a sort of agreement, which is good enough for me.

"Great. I'll be back in five minutes." Ginger starts to follow me, but I turn back and command her to stay before rushing down the hill.

The kitchen is empty: Jack's gone and I can hear my mom walking around upstairs. My eye catches the wine bottle sitting in the recycling bin near the door. Wow, that was fast.

In the tiny first-floor bathroom, Nurse Mom's got drugs galore, although nothing prescription. Just the usual OTC: Tylenol, Advil, aspirin, Aleve, a few sleeping pills, some Benadryl. All in giant white bottles without childproof caps. I grab five of everything and then grab a

Coke on my way through the kitchen.

I pause with one hand on the door. Priya said she was going back tonight. Not to her "home planet," of course, but her real home, wherever it is. But what if she's wrong? Like she was before?

Or what if she's totally bats and there's no one coming for her at all, even though she thinks there is? She can't stay out in the field again by herself.

I could leave Ginger with her, but that dog's no Lassie. She's more likely to run away from trouble than to save anyone from it. And what if it rains before her ride comes?

In the front hall closet I find an old tent from the weekend Brian and I were Cub Scouts. Frankly we weren't much interested in troop activities, but we really wanted to go camping. Or we thought we did. After a miserably cold weekend in the woods, we decided we'd rather make forts indoors where we could watch TV and raid the fridge.

I knock aside boxes of crap until I find the nylon tent with a foldable aluminum frame. It's small but better than nothing.

When I get to the field, Priya is sitting up, her legs stretched in front of her, notebook on her lap. I try to get a glimpse of the page she's reading, but her hand covers most of the writing.

She glances up with a quizzical smile as if I surprised her by coming back.

"Voilà." I open my palm and display a rainbow of pills:

orange aspirin, pink Benadryl, brown Advil, red-white-and-blue Tylenol, blue Aleve.

"Pretty," she says. "What are they?"

"Medicine. For your headache."

And now her eyes open a little wider, her memory sparked. "Oh yes."

"What do you want? Aspirin, Advil?"

She stares forlornly at the drugs and then holds her head again. "This pain will not go away. Not with those."

"Are you sure? My mom gets migraines, you know, and she wants to throw up but she takes, like, a bunch of this shit and feels a lot better."

She cradles her head in her palm. "Thank you, Matthew."

"Don't you even want to try? Personally I'm a Tylenol guy."

She looks at the pills, at me, and then back again. "Which is Tylenol?"

I pick out two of the oblong-shaped pills and place them in the palm of her hand, and then open the Coke for her. It pops loudly in the silence of the empty field, startling both of us. "Tylenol, sugar, and caffeine. How can you go wrong?"

She hesitates before swallowing the drugs, sipping carefully from the can as if she doesn't want to touch her lips to the metal.

I unfold the tent for her, snapping the lightweight rods together and sliding them through the ends of the nylon covering. Considering I did this only once in my life, I manage to figure it out pretty fast. Priya watches, fascinated.

"Voilà," I say for the second time, not sure when I got so sophisticated as to regularly use French words.

"This is . . . ?"

"A tent. For you."

Priya runs her hands along the smooth edges, peeks inside. "It is very charming. Thank you. It's a . . . ?"

"Tent. A tent."

She flips a page in her notebook and scratches her pen across the paper.

"You sleep inside it," I tell her, demonstrating. I don't quite fit: either my head or my feet stick out. "Well, you're small. You can curl up." I crawl back out and hold the flap up for her. She doesn't budge.

"Okay, well. There you go. Now you have a place to sleep and I don't have to worry anymore. Okay? Okay." I stand up and wipe the grass off my pants. "Come on, Ginger."

I wave to Priya as Ginger and I start down the hill. "Have a nice trip home, wherever you live."

"My planet is near Gliese 581c," she replies.

"Yep. Near Gliese 581c. Good luck with that." I shake my head. The girl is a wack job. Beautiful, yes. Sweet, it would seem so, and smart, but . . .

Not an alien. And therefore as crazy as a loon.

Inside I wander through the house, shutting off the

lights as I go. I should feel relief that we're done, Priya and I. If her ride comes, if it doesn't. Doesn't matter. I have my phone back and *I'm* done.

Then I run to the side door and double check that it's open. Just in case.

2:27 A.M.

I pull a chair up to the window in the guest room. This and my mom's room are the only ones that face the space field. From here, if I use my old G.I. Joe binoculars, I can see Priya.

I thought I was done—I mean, I know I *am* done—but I couldn't sleep knowing she was out there. I tossed and turned and well, here I am.

Keeping an eye on her. That's all I'm doing. I'm not stalking her. I'm not spying on her. I'm making sure nothing happens to her. She's a girl all alone in a field. Someone unscrupulous, someone who doesn't have her best interests at heart, might try to take advantage of her. Or, what's more likely is she gets bitten by a million mosquitoes or twists her ankle in the dark. I'm here for that, too.

I feel a little silly using the binocs. They're kiddie-size, from a party Brian had when he was six and big into action figures. We used to play Search and Rescue in the creek and sometimes G.I. Joe would rescue Emily's Barbie while riding his surfboard.

You didn't know Joe could surf? Oh, Joe can do many things. Rescuing pretty blond dolls with big boobs and high heels is his specialty, though, and many afternoons were spent pulling Barbie from deep water or the crooks of tree branches.

The binoculars barely cover my eyes, but if I hold them and squint, I can just make out Priya in the field. She sits there, legs stretched in front of her, hands in her lap, chin to the sky. There's an awkward, colt-like quality to the way she sits. I'm used to girls like Emily, who twine their legs at their knees and ankles, who hug their legs to their chest. Even my mom can't sit still. She's often crossing and uncrossing her knees, sitting with her feet pressed together, curling her legs under her butt.

But Priya just sits there, motionless. I realize I have never seen her walk. I have seen her stand and sit and lie back on the ground, but I wonder what she looks like when she walks. Does she strut like a supermodel? Tiptoe like a dancer? Does she run, jog, sprint? Does she pump her arms by her sides or hold them close to her waist?

I stare at Priya and imagine her moving. Imagine her reaching her arms to me, wrapping them around my neck and back, and pulling me close to her. Her legs pressed to mine, her lips on my cheek, her breath in my ear.

She'll call me Matthew and I'll laugh and tickle her until she calls me Matty. And . . .

She's not your personal porn channel. I take a breath and look away, give my fired-up hormones a chance to think of something else and calm down, for god's sake.

I wonder if Brian's tried to reach me. I grab my phone and bring it back to the window. The Wi-Fi's lousy all over the house but there's some kind of signal here. I tap the screen and see about a dozen messages. I don't even bother reading them.

Yo, I type.

Sup dude?

Um . . . I type the truth: *girl's back*

Yaaaaassss

She's

I start to type "crazy" and stop. I try "alien" and stop.

Whut???

She's going home tonight

And as soon as I type that, I feel my ribs ache like someone punched me hard. Yes, she's going home, wherever that is, and I won't ever see her again.

And I want to. I really, really want to.

What's her name again? Brian texts back.

"Priya," I say aloud. "Priya. Priya." It feels weird on my tongue. I can imagine Brian goofing on her: "What is she, a car? Gets good gas mileage, har, har."

Before I can respond, another message: *don't forget cat*

Oh crap, that's right. I told the Aokis I'd take in the mail and shit while they were gone. They have a cat too. Emily's cat. Super finicky. The only cat I know of that won't eat canned food. It has to be prepared fresh every day, which is why they need a sitter whenever they go away.

What cat?

Dude!! Em would kill u

Little does Brian know Em has already killed me. We were stealthy in our hookup on grad night. No one knew but us. Neither of us was sure what Brian would do if he found out.

Yeah yeah cat got it

Dude cool

We spend another minute goofing around until Brian's mom calls him away and I'm back on my own.

I reach for my laptop and open Google, type Priya's name into the search bar, just to see what comes up.

Not much, as it turns out. It's the name of a bunch of films, a popular sitcom character, and an Indian restaurant fifty miles away. But locally? Nothing. Even when I search Google news, I don't come up with her name anywhere.

That's a good sign, right? That means nothing's wrong.

She's not an escaped mental patient. She's not a killer on the run.

Except I don't know her full name. Or if Priya is really her name at all. I really don't know anything about her.

I groan and pick up the binocs again. She's leaning against the tent now, her face tilted up at the sky, and that makes me smile. At least it's good for something.

Is she really waiting for a lift from the other side of the universe? She sure thinks so.

I take to Google again and this time search the skies. Maybe a comet's on its way, scheduled to pass through our atmosphere soon, or a meteor shower. People like my dad's blog followers, who believe in aliens and interstellar space conspiracies, are usually big into astronomy, too, and events like passing comets or the Perseid meteor shower give them the crazy idea that something or someone is coming for them.

But at the NASA site, there's no news of any upcoming happenings in the skies, nothing that screams, *The aliens are coming!* Of course, that phrase would never be on a government site. It would be on . . .

. . . do I dare? I know the address by heart, although I wish I didn't.

www.reallifewithufos.com

Dad's crazy-ass website. You've seen it. Or you've seen one like it. Or maybe you've seen a thousand like it.

Black background, tiny yellow-and-white lettering, lots of exclamation points. Every headline is BIG NEWS!!! Every follower includes the words *UFO* or *conspiracy* in his or her Twitter handle. Every photo of a flying saucer or a gray-faced blobby ET includes the caption "Not to scale" or "Artist's rendering" to make sure we know it's not real—but it sure as hell could be and *we all know it*.

On one side is a list of links to DJ's favorite sites: legit ones like NASA and ESA and all the observatories in the country but also the crazies like We Believe, I Was Taken, We Are Not Alone, and so on. On the other side is his Twitter feed, a constant stream of posts and comments from his followers.

His blog, *A Star Is Born*, is smack in the middle of the page. He's got 304 subscribers, most of whom love to comment using GIFs and strings of emoji.

Yeah.

I never minded my dad's interest in aliens and astronomy. It was what we did together; it was our family legacy. Dad always told me the stars were our destiny—we were made of star stuff, like Carl Sagan famously said, only us more so than everyone else. We searched the skies with our telescopes and charted the planets in the galaxy. We high-fived whenever a new exoplanet was discovered, another possible Earth. DJ and Junior, father and son.

The blog was ours for a long time too. There were pictures of *us*. Pictures of *me*. Our house, our dog, our field.

Our telescopes. And it was fine and it was fun and it was ours.

But then, when I was in ninth grade, it suddenly morphed into something else. I remember I'd been busy with Brian and Em a lot back then: Bri and I were new to high school and there was a lot more work to do. And Mom kept pushing me ("Face facts, Matty, you need a scholarship if you want to go to college"). So I hadn't been paying attention to Dad and the blog.

I knew he always wanted to bring more people to our small town, to make the field a tourist attraction, but this was different. This was more *out there.* He was starting to appeal to the wack jobs, the Tin Foil Hat society. They had rediscovered the episode of a reality TV show about our town that was made in 1990 and they began pushing him for more.

And to my huge and utter astonishment, he complied. He gave it all back to them—and beyond. He gave up on "DJ and Junior" and spent more and more time with the online crazies.

I notice the blog hasn't been updated since before Dad left. His last entry—about the potential for life existing on icy Pluto (#ibelieve)—sheds no light on where he went or with whom.

When I look at the comments his followers are leaving on Twitter, though, I see *they* care.

@braintrust: *DJ!! Did they take u??*

@fmulder: *u're not talkin. wr r u???*

@therealdana: *dude, in town? gotta c u!!!*

On and on, names and dates and places, people worried he was taken, people celebrating he was taken. Everyone believes. Every. Single. One.

I don't. I don't believe at all. What I believe is that he encouraged people who were probably on the edge of sanity to take a giant flying leap off the cliff. He wrote stupid nonsense about aliens and life on other planets and what it must be like to travel through the stars at warp speed. Half of the tech shit was real; half was cribbed from Syfy channel. I'll bet he doesn't even know which is which anymore. What's worse, though, is that he doesn't care.

"What does it matter, Junior?" he'd say with a shrug. "It makes them happy. They have dull lives and they want to cheer themselves up."

"With conspiracy theories?"

"It's harmless. They're harmless. It's just for fun."

I think of Priya out in the field. Is this just fun for her? Is this harmless?

I close the site, shut off my computer, and take one last look at her through the binoculars. She's asleep. A quick glance at the digital clock on the bedside table relaxes me a bit. Only a few more hours of being vigilant, of watching over her until daylight comes.

Or until she gets a lift home.

DAY THREE

8:32 A.M.

Morning comes with a bang. Literally a huge crash that jolts me awake.

"Mom? You okay?"

The last syllable is cut off by another thunk of metal against stone and a "Shit!"

She must have dropped something on the kitchen floor. For a split second I forget why I'm sleeping in a chair in the guest bedroom and then the binoculars with G.I. Joe's logo on them remind me. I peek through the window and see Priya awake and standing, her back to the house, her arms at her sides.

Seeing her jump-starts my blood. I stretch for a

moment and shake out the kinks in my legs and neck and head downstairs.

Mom has started to make the coffee—except the grounds are all over the floor. Looks like she was reaching for the can on the top shelf, knocked over the toaster, and dropped the can.

"Shit," she says when I walk in, barefoot.

"And a happy shit to you too."

"Ugh! I am not in the mood for this crap." She pinches the skin between her eyes and winces. "I need coffee. Lots. Make it, please." She holds out the half-empty can and ignores the grounds on the floor. "And don't let Ginger eat that. She'll get sick."

I salute her. "Aye, aye, Cap'n."

"Not today, Matty. Not today."

I resist the urge to say something snarky about her hangover because she'd probably smack me. I do the coffee thing, the dog thing, and scoot my mom out the door with her giant Thermos and a promise that yes, I will clean up the kitchen; yes, I will check on the Aokis' house; and no, I don't mind if Jack comes over for dinner after work.

All I can think about is Priya. I am determined to get the truth and get her home.

I grab some Cokes and toast, because breakfast, and when I get to the field, Priya is in the same place as when I woke up. Dangling from one hand is her notebook.

"Hey," I greet her when she turns. She looks at me oddly,

as if she can't quite place me. "You okay?"

Her nod is slow and steady and her eyes dart from my head to my feet. When she sees Ginger trot up the slope, her face beams. She bends down and accepts a warm snuggle from my dog.

In the daylight, she takes my breath away. The sun's rays sink into her skin, as if it were absorbing every molecule and making it contrast richly with her pale blue shirt. Her hair shimmers like a mirror, a brighter white than it was at night, the black under it a liquid sheet of ink. Everything about her is *more* than it was at night. More brilliant. More defined.

"Sleep all right? How'd you like the tent?"

"Tent, yes. I don't need to sleep."

"Uh, well, you did. I saw you."

"You were watching me?"

"Um . . . not really watching, just . . ." I mentally stumble through all the inappropriate things I'm probably implying: stalker, predator . . . what says *I just want you to be safe*?

"Although that wasn't necessary, thank you."

"You're still here," I say. "I mean, I thought you were leaving for real last night."

Priya's lips twist and she shakes her head. "This is a puzzle for me. I have recalculated the projections several times."

I take a deep breath. "Has it occurred to you that maybe you *aren't* an alien?"

"I am not an alien, as you say. I am from another planet."

I feel a grin and I don't want to smile, but okay, I do. "Well, here we'd call you an alien."

"If you feel the need to define me, then that is what I am."

I pop open two cans of Coke and hand her one. "Toast?"

Instead of getting angry and upset, like my dad would if I called him on something, a "fact" about aliens or Area 51, she merely gazes at me. "Why can't you accept what I'm saying as truth, Matthew?"

"Matty."

"Matthew."

"Matty—look, why don't you just prove it to me?"

"Prove what?"

Oh my god, she's exasperating. "Prove that you're an alien. Prove you're from Gliese 581c."

"*Near* Gliese 581c."

"Near. Far. Whatever." I chomp a bite of buttery toast, and crumbs spray over my shirt. "Prove it to me."

When she smiles, my stomach cinches up. *Stop that!* I want to shout. *Stop giving me a mini heart attack whenever you look me in the eye.*

"How can I prove it?"

"Do you have green blood? Or two hearts?"

She looks up at the sun. "No. No."

"Then I guess you're not an alien."

"Matthew—"

"Matty."

"Do you only believe in things that can be proved? Aren't there things that can't be proved that you believe in?"

"If you're trying to talk to me about faith, that's religion, which is way different than science and fact."

"Is it? Can you prove gravity?"

I take my shoe off, hold it above my head, then let it drop. It falls to the ground with a gentle thump. "Gravity. Next."

"But how do you prove *that* is what caused your shoe to fall?"

"Oh, wow. Are you one of those 'gravity is only a theory' people? I've heard of you all, but I've never met one of you before."

A theory, as we all know from grade school, is what scientists call just about everything because science never proves anything. It can't. Nothing is absolute. But the average person thinks "theory" means it's a whim, a fantasy, a passing fancy.

"Gravity can't be proved, like nothing in science can be absolutely proved," Priya says with an impish grin.

"Reading my mind again?"

She shrugs. "You're easily readable. The thoughts just jump from your head"—she taps my temple with her fingertip and then her own—"into mine."

Does she also know how hot I think she is? Can she tell?

"I'm a pragmatist, okay?" I tell her, making my voice sound gruff. "I gotta see it to believe it."

A smile and light laugh dismiss my concern. Her eyes shine in the sun, full of pity for me, a disappointment that I don't believe what she does. I've seen that look before.

I don't let her deter me, as charming as her laugh is, as infectious as her smile may be. "You're still here," I say for the thousandth time. "No ride last night."

"That is unfortunate but correct."

I pointedly glance around the empty field. "No ride this morning."

"It is daytime," she says with a sly smile.

"Only nighttime pickups, huh? It's tricky to maneuver a ship at night."

"Trickier to see them too. Night landings are less disruptive for you."

I point to my chest. "For me?"

If she's frustrated by my questions, she doesn't show it. "For humans. If we landed during daylight, there would be far, far more problems."

"Oh yes, nighttime landings . . . nobody would notice that at all. Like, *at all.* I think all our observatories are closed at night. Too hard to see stuff." She doesn't react to my sarcasm. "So, if you are an alien, where's your mother ship? Running late? Stuck in space traffic? What would that be anyway, a comet's tail? Meteor shower?"

"It is *my* fault."

"How is it your fault?"

"My calculations were not precise," she says. "I thought last night was correct, but perhaps it's tonight."

"Maybe you won't ever get picked up."

"I will, that is a definite. I *am* going home."

We are both quiet for a long moment. I can hear traffic far off in the distance, a car horn, a truck on the single main drag of our small town. Finally, Priya breaks the silence. "Very well. I will give you evidence."

I let my shoulders rise and fall. "I'm all ears."

She pulls out her notebook and flips past a few pages with exceptionally neat handwriting, almost like it was typed. At the end of the book I see pages of diagrams and charts, not unlike Dad's star charts. "This is the calculation we use to plan the route the ship will take from our planet, through the wormhole, and into your solar system." She taps her finger on a complex algorithm that I swear uses the infinity symbol.

I shake my head. "Priya, I wouldn't know if that's real or not. I'm not an astrophysicist."

"Neither am I." She holds my gaze, drawing me closer to her with every blink of her deep-set eyes. We are so alone out here, and I feel the weight of the Universe around us. "I'm merely a data collector."

I want to laugh, to make a joke of it, but she is deadly serious. My words choke in my throat and I swallow them back with a nod. "Data collector. Okay."

"My planet, my people, we have a . . . a . . ." Her thin brow snakes into a question mark. "A hunger? Yes, a hunger for knowledge. There is so much we do not know." Her eyes find mine again. "You share that too. You want to know things. About life. About your Universe."

About you.

I allow my shoulders to shrug. She's right, sort of. At least it used to be true, back when my dad believed in actual science instead of all the fakery and BS.

"I would like to show you something." She points at my dad's workshop. "I need what's in there."

"Uh, okay."

Ginger follows on our heels as we head to the basement. The air temperature cools with every step we take.

I lead Priya through the underground tunnel and stop at the midway point like I always do. I do my thing because I have to, pretending to hold up a ton of earth above my head, feigning strain and flexing my puny muscles.

"Ta-da!"

Priya laughs politely.

"Oh, you think you can do better?"

She grins, a little cocky if you ask me, and then puts her hands on the ground.

"Yep, that's awesome," I say with some snark thrown in. I do a slow-clap but she ignores me and kicks her legs up in the air so her feet are on the ceiling of the tunnel.

"Whoa, nice!" I say. "Is that how they stand wherever you're from?"

Her bare legs pump up and down so it looks like she's walking on the ceiling, which is kind of cute and makes me smile. As soon as she starts to move, though, her hair brushes the dirt floor and her skirt flips up, revealing a very small pair of pink panties.

Oh my god.

I turn my head but I can't avoid seeing her T-shirt falling to her shoulders and pulling down over her bra. Which is also pink.

I feel all the blood leave my face and brain and every other important organ and find its way straight to my crotch. I couldn't blush if I wanted to. There's nothing left up there to blush with.

Just then I hear Priya giggle, and that breaks my focus on her near-naked body.

Calm down, Matty. She's just a girl.

And I have no idea how much longer she can hold herself up on those spindly arms of hers.

"Help?" she says in a small voice.

Right. Not very long. I grab hold of her calves and keep her upright. "Gotcha." Her skin is soft and pliable in my hands; my fingers knead her delicate muscles without even trying. Her legs bend and she tucks her head under her arms, somersaulting to the ground to finish with her knees pulled up in front of her chest and her hands on her shins. She grins up at me. "Ta-da!"

I pull her to standing. "Is everyone a gymnast where you're from?" I tease her.

Priya pushes me away playfully. "No. And we don't walk on our hands." She heads for the workshop, steadying her walk with one hand against the tunnel wall. "We're like you."

My mind pictures her pink underwear and bra and I think, *Uh, no, you're not.*

At the door to the shop, Priya enters first and goes straight to the workbench. Her finger traces one of the star charts on the wall above the wooden bench and she murmurs a few words.

"What did you say?"

"Gliese 581c is crossed out? Why?"

"It's not habitable."

She laughs to herself and shakes her head. "So you think."

"It *is* habitable?"

She rolls her eyes. "The inhabitants of Gliese 581c certainly think so."

"What?"

"Although they do not call it that, naturally."

"Naturally."

She tilts her head to one side and leans closer to me. The air heats up between us. "Are you teasing me, Matthew?"

She adds with a lopsided smile, "Again?"

Holy shit. Is she flirting with me?

"I, uh, I . . ." I'm not good at recognizing flirting. Emily's told me a million times I'm dense. She's right. I am. So what do I do?

I force a scowl. "Now why on *earth* would I tease you, Priya?" I wink exaggeratedly. "See what I did there? I said 'earth' 'cause we were talking about other planets."

She blinks once, very slowly and deliberately. "You are *not* as clever as you think you are."

I sigh. "I don't think I'm clever at all."

Priya turns back to the wall and finds another chart, the one that shows the the orbits of the Gliese 581 planetary system. Her finger taps the glossy poster. "My planet is not on this star map. It's much too small to be seen."

I snort. "Doubt that. NASA has some serious telescopes. And the observatory in Philly? They've got some pretty good refractors." I pull a stool up to the bench and sit down. "Somebody somewhere has seen your planet."

Wait. Did I just say . . . "your planet"? I wave my hand across the air as if I could erase what I just said. Because I sure as hell don't mean it.

"So what did you want in here?"

"Your telescope." Priya runs to it, nearly embracing it.

"I, um . . . I haven't used it in a while. Not sure if it works."

"If I had a telescope, I'd use it every night."

I shrug. "Not really my thing anymore. Stars, planets . . . who cares?"

"I don't understand," she says, shaking her head. "You have a telescope. You have star charts. You live next to *this field*, which is filled with interstellar energy." She gestures toward the small square-paned window facing the weeping willows. "And yet you claim to have no interest in any of it." She crosses her arms at her waist. "I don't believe *you*."

She stares so hard at me, it should be laughable. Like when a little kid is trying to beat you at a staring contest. Eyes wide and bulging, chin jutted forward, that tapered jaw and dimpled chin, set and determined.

I squirm under her gaze and glance away. "I don't have time for that crap. I have school and my friends and . . ."

What, Matty? What do you have? Smoking weed and riding a dirt bike? That's all I have. I don't do sports. Don't play an instrument or sing or write. No chess club or drama club or Model United Nations.

I've never had a real girlfriend. Not unless you count hooking up once with Emily. And I don't. Why should I? She sure as hell doesn't.

"But the telescope—"

"Is my dad's."

"Not yours?"

"Not mine."

"I think it's yours."

"You're wrong." I try to say it firmly, but my voice shakes.

Priya forces me to meet her gaze. "If you don't care, then you won't mind if I use it."

"You gonna look for your ride?"

"I'm going to show you my home," she says soberly. "I miss it."

"Oh. Yeah. Okay. Do whatever you want."

"Thank you."

The sun is hours from setting. There's far too much daylight to see any stars at all, let alone a planet in another solar system. I watch Priya stare at the star chart. Her homesickness inhabits her entire body: her shoulders roll forward, her hands twist in her lap, and tears fill her eyes.

I have no idea what it's like to miss home. I've never been anywhere that wasn't in my home state. Except for Disney World. We went there the summer I was seven. I don't really remember much about it except it rained the whole day, which meant we got to ride Space Mountain a dozen times. Otherwise, my world—my planet—has been my corner of Pennsylvania.

God, that's boring.

My phone buzzes in my back pocket. A text from Brian.

Dude how's the cat?

Oh crap. Em's cat.

I quickly type back: *what cat haha*

"Priya, I have to go out for a bit. I gotta take care of some things. You gonna be okay here?"

She blinks. "I have been fine for days. Why would that status change?"

Now I do laugh. "Good point."

When she blinks again, though, her eyelids appear heavy and weighted. She looks suddenly exhausted. "Do you want to lie down? You can go upstairs, if you want."

"No, no. This is fine." She reaches a hand to the floor, steadying herself as she slumps to the concrete. "I will stay here. With the stars." Her fingers trail up the legs of the telescope's tripod.

"Okay, sure, um, I'll leave Ginger with you and the door open. If you need to go upstairs, get a drink or whatever . . ."

"I will be fine, Matthew. Go take care of the cat."

My gut flutters. How did she—?

My phone. She had to have seen the text from Brian.

She. Is. Not. An. Alien.

I still don't know where she's from or why she's here. I take one last glance at her sitting on the floor, her legs stretched in front of her and her head resting uncomfortably against the wall.

Someone is missing this girl. But who? And where are they?

2:14 P.M.

I know the Aokis' three-story house like it was my own. The front porch has two wide planks that collapse if you stand on both of them at once. The tree outside Brian's bedroom on the third floor is totally climbable. The tree outside Emily's room is totally not.

I know where Brian stashes his weed and his snacks. I know where Emily hides her diary. No, I've never read her private journals, but I have partaken of a Kit Kat or two when Brian wasn't looking.

I know the trick to opening the attic door and the best way to crank up the heat in the wintertime. I've put sandbags outside the basement door during spring floods and I've pulled down icicles from the rain gutters.

Most important of all? I know how to hook up the Xbox, which is exactly what I do after I bring in the mail and feed Emily's cat. It takes me twenty minutes to chop the fresh vegetables and chicken and blend it all up in an actual blender before scooping it into her special ceramic bowl. Stupid cat.

Boo's litter box in the laundry room needs to be emptied, but I'm waiting until the air clears. Just one day with the windows and doors closed and the stench of cat urine has permeated the air. I can't get within yards of the box without gagging.

I was last in this house about four days ago, but that was with Brian. There's something eerie and disquieting about being in another family's home without them. While you might know facts about them, I'm reminded that sometimes you don't really know other people at all.

Like my dad.

Like Emily.

Like, who could have guessed Emily would stomp on my heart after we hooked up? Was it so awful to even consider dating me? Am I gross? Do I not use enough deodorant? I crushed on that girl for a year. Granted, she had no clue about that, but couldn't she have spent a few more seconds crafting a response to me? Did she have to say no so fast?

I know she had a good time with me—like, I *know*

it—but it wasn't enough. I wasn't enough.

In the kitchen, I find a note from Mrs. Aoki for me:

> *Hi, Matty! Thanks for watching the house and looking out for Boo. Mr. Aoki's insulin will arrive by FedEx and MUST go in the fridge when it comes! (Help yourself to anything in there, except the insulin—ha!)*

Ha.

> *Please don't leave the doors or windows open! Hugs!*

I check the fridge but the Aokis did a good job of clearing out most of the perishables before their trip to Gran's. Usually, they have a kitchen filled with food, enough for the four of them with plenty of extras in case friends come over or they have a party, which they often do in the summer. Mr. and Mrs. Aoki have always been "the neighbors who host parties," going all the way back to when they first moved in and people were skeptical of them.

Skeptical or afraid?

But parties were the ice-breakers, and that was all because of my dad. He was the one who suggested they do something to let people get to know them.

"You're new is all" is what my dad told Brian's dad. "You just need to show them you're no different from them. We're all the same."

And they did. They had a big bash and my mom and dad went and sure enough, the neighborhood embraced them. It was the first of a long-standing tradition of summer parties at the Aokis'.

My dad was right. He had an old-fashioned charm and a sincere interest in helping others and he knew what would win people over. I guess he still does. I think my mom would agree, although we might not like *who* he's charming these days.

I fling open the back door, first making sure Boo the cat isn't anywhere around, and let the fresh air fill the kitchen. The backyard has a set of patio furniture and an old trampoline. I can't remember the last time we jumped on it, but it was pretty popular at the Aokis' summer parties for a while.

Damn, their barbecue potlucks were always the best, with every family bringing something to grill. It was at their Fourth of July party last summer that I fell in love with Em.

After all those years of knowing her as just my friend, just Brian's mostly serious older sister, I saw her in a different light—the light of the fireflies and holiday sparklers.

When Mom and Dad and I arrived that afternoon with our corn and chicken, Em was wearing a yellow sundress with a matching yellow headband, and she kept kicking off her flip-flops to run through the sprinklers with the little kids she babysat for. They loved her.

And so, apparently, did a senior named Jared Lloyd, who played baseball and was also at the party. He was a *guy* guy, with a husky voice and a varsity letter, and I was just Brian's friend who couldn't drive yet. Jared jumped in there with her, exuberant and joyful, and they held hands with the little kids and they were both so happy.

I wanted that happy.

I wanted that joy, that love.

I wanted Emily. I wanted her for a whole year, and when I finally got my chance on grad night, I took it and I couldn't let go. It might have been one night in 365 for her, but for me it was everything. It was the *only* night.

A cool breeze blows in from the yard where the skies have darkened, threatening rain. My thoughts rush to Priya, who is, I hope, asleep in the workshop with Ginger. I still have to wait for the FedEx guy, but I should have plenty of time to get her out of the house before Mom comes home.

I grab a soda and some chips that are on the edge of stale and tuck myself into the couch to play some Xbox while I wait. The wind rattles the panes and up pops Boo, Emily's silky-soft tuxedo cat. She gracefully hops from the floor to the coffee table and then to me. She takes a quick disdainful sniff at my chips before she curls her tail around my arm while I shoot the bad guys on the screen.

6:10 P.M.

I died fifteen times in Call of Duty before FedEx finally arrived. The driver must have thought I was a lunatic when I grabbed the box from him and slammed the door in his face.

I can't believe how late it is, but I'm pretty sure I can . . .

Crap.

Jack's Mustang is in the garage in Dad's old spot.

Crap.

Mom and Jack are in the kitchen, sitting in the same chairs at the kitchen table they were in last night. They've even got a fresh bottle of wine. I cross my fingers they've gotten through enough of it that they don't notice me walk in and head for the . . .

"Hey, kiddo!" Jack calls to me.

Crap.

Mom's got a sour expression on her face but Jack is all shiny buzz cut and peachy skin.

"Oh hey, Jack. Nice wheels."

"Thanks. It's a convertible." He turns on the car-salesman smile, but since it has no place to go, no one to land on but me, it quickly fades.

Aaannnd, we're done. How fast can I get out of here and check the workshop for Priya? "Um, so what are we eating for dinner tonight?"

Mom's eyes widen as she realizes the table has only alcohol on it. "I'm sorry, Matty. Dinner just—it slipped my mind."

"Yeah, food's so rarely on my mind too."

"Order something, okay? I'm not in a mood to cook."

"Yeah, okay, pizza good?"

Mom shrugs. Uncle Jack shrugs. Lost in their mutual pity.

Anger washes over me like a hot, red wave. *They were losers!* I want to scream, shaking them by their shoulders and waking them up. That bottle of wine should be a cel-ebration of Carol and Dad leaving. Don't they see that? They're not *dead.* They're just *not here.* And we're all better off because of it!

But I say none of this. "Half pepperoni, half mushroom?"

When they don't respond, I add, "Side of cockroaches? Couple orders of fried snake balls?"

"Whatever you want is fine with me." My mother pours another inch of wine into her glass and glances sideways at Jack. Obviously there's more they want to say, but I'm here. I caused a disturbance in the Force.

Fine. Whatever. I order the pizza and start for the basement—until my mother's voice stops me.

"Matty, hey?"

"Yeah?" *I found a girl in your dad's shop. . . .*

"Where's the dog?"

"Oh, uh, she's outside." I pause, my breath held.

"Oh . . . okay."

That's it? I don't know why I was worried. I hurry to the basement and run through the tunnel to the workshop.

Empty. No Priya. No Ginger. And no telescope. Upstairs in the guest room, I check the field with my cheap binoculars and find girl and dog resting comfortably.

Okay, now I can exhale.

And wait for pizza.

6:45 P.M.

"... Hollywood, I guess," I hear my uncle say as I run downstairs to grab the pizza. I waited to come down until they paid for it, naturally.

"Not Roswell?" My mother's voice is heavy with sarcasm. "Or Cheyenne Mountain?"

"I can't picture Carol anywhere near there," Jack says, bewildered. "When was she ever interested in alien bullshit? Did I miss something? A sign?"

God, these two are morons. *Let it go. Let. Them. Go.*

"I don't want to contact the cops," Jack says. "Should I? Do we need to wait until three days have passed or something like that?"

Stop talking like it matters. It doesn't.

Fortunately the smell of fresh pizza keeps me from blasting them both with my opinions. Two pizza boxes sit smack in the middle of the table—unopened as I knew they would be.

"Um, hey? Are you finished with the pizza?" I ask Mom and Jack. I point to the table and they both look at me as if they never heard the word before, and then at the boxes as if they had no idea how they got there. Even though they just paid for them.

Jack furrows his brow. "I'm done. Are you, Lorna?"

My mother bobs her head. "Take as much as you want, sweetheart."

Sweetheart? Okay, let's put the wine down and take a breath.

I grab both boxes and snag a couple of Cokes from the fridge.

Before I can leave, though, I'm stopped again—this time by my uncle.

I sigh, not even trying to hide my exasperation. "You changed your mind," I say. "You want the pizza."

A glimpse of the car-salesman smile fades in a heartbeat. "Did you, uh, did you find your dad's box? Was it in the shop?"

I sharpen the edges of my voice, make sure both of them hear the no-bullshit tone in it. "No. It's all gone. His whole workshop is empty."

"You're sure you didn't—"

"Nothing's there." I swing myself out the door before I get any more stupid questions. They're so concerned about the deed to the farm that they don't realize that it means nothing to my dad. The fact that the box is missing is irrelevant. He probably took it and didn't even realize what was in it. What *really* means he's gone is the missing telescope. *That's* how you know he's not coming back. Don't they get it?

Up at the field, Ginger guards Priya, who is sitting on the ground with her feet tucked inside the tent, notebook on her lap. The telescope is on the tripod, aimed at the sky, which is getting darker because of cloud cover. The air is heavy and humid, ripe for rain. Priya's not going to get her view of the stars tonight.

As if to underscore my thought, thunder rumbles in the distance.

"Um, hey—"

Priya's face opens into a smile. "I brought the telescope," she says. "I hope you don't mind."

I cast a critical eye at the green bubble of liquid on the tripod. "Looks level to me. Nice job setting it up."

"Thank you."

"But you know it's going to rain, right? In about . . ." I lick my forefinger and hold it up to the wind. "Ten—no, five seconds."

Priya mimics me and it looks like she's politely hailing

a waiter. "I do not understand. Does your finger control the weather?"

"Ha, no. It's just a thing my granddad used to do. Old-school weather prediction."

She nods. "Ah, I see." She picks up her pen, about to jot a note, and then stops.

"I guess it's not important enough to collect, huh?"

She shakes her head. "I don't believe we can use that, no."

Thunder rumbles again, louder, closer, and Ginger walks around my legs in a circle. She's an outdoor dog except in the rain and snow, when she turns into a giant lap dog.

"Seriously. Rain. Two seconds." I grab the telescope and thrust it into Priya's arms, then push her into the tent, following with the pizza. Naturally, Ginger barrels in too, positioning herself between Priya, me, and the pizza. It's a tight squeeze and my head keeps grazing the aluminum rod holding it up, but who cares? I've got sixteen slices of mouthwatering pizza from the best joint in town.

Oh man, the scent of melting mozzarella and garlic and onions is overpowering. I can't wait. I pull out a cheesy slice and flip the triangle over and onto a second slice, forming a pizza sandwich. I fold that in half and shove one end into my mouth. Grease oozes from the folded corners and I lean over the box to let it drip onto the white cardboard. Ginger whines, so I give her a bite of crust with some sauce on it.

"Holy crap, this is *so* good," I say, still chewing. I had

no idea how hungry I was. Priya stares at me for a long moment, almost as if she doesn't remember what pizza—or hunger, or *me*—is.

I offer her the box. "Cheese on this one. And that's got pepperoni and mushrooms. Oh, and here are some drinks."

I open the box and watch, incredulously, as she does exactly what I did: she takes one slice, flips it over on top of another, folds it in half, and then stuffs it into her mouth.

Okay, that is seriously awesome. I don't think I've ever seen a girl do that, not even Emily.

"How do you not drip oil all over you?" I ask, amazed. "I think my dog was expecting to have something to lick up."

Priya finishes the huge bite, smacking her lips like a total pizza fiend, following it with a long slug of the Coke—yet she's still careful not to touch her mouth to the can.

"Do you like it?"

"I have never had this."

"Never?" I can't believe anyone who's our age *not* having had pizza. Maybe they haven't had *good* pizza, but none at all?

"No, none at all," she says, answering my unasked question. It's still jarring, but I'm kind of getting used to it. We finish our slices and then Priya says, "I would like some more, please."

"Yeah? Okay, I'll take one too."

Again, she sandwiches two slices together and I do the same. We wolf these down in slightly more time than it takes to say "More, please." And just like that, an entire eight-slice pizza pie vanishes.

More lip smacking, more Coke, and when she's done, I spot a tiny bit of sauce on Priya's cheeks. Two swipes of red like smeared lipstick. It's so adorable that I want to take a picture of her. Would that be weird?

Before I can do anything, though, Ginger jumps up and licks the sauce off Priya's face. She falls back against the tent, her elbows digging into the ground.

"Ginger! What the hell are you doing?" I pull the dog away from Priya and shake my finger in her face. "Bad dog. No pizza for you."

Too late I remember Priya's sensitivity. She covers my hand with hers and pulls it away from Ginger. "Please don't scold her. Her food should not be withheld because of her poor behavior."

I laugh. "Okay, okay. Why don't you feed her?" I grab the pizza box with the pepperoni. "She loves cheese, hates mushrooms."

Priya pinches a gooey blob of cheese from a slice and holds it out to Ginger, who inhales it before she can blink. "Oh! She's very hungry!"

"She's always hungry. She would eat both pizzas, burp, and then eat two more."

Priya's laugh is like wind chimes as she pulls an entire slice from the box and feeds it to my dog bite by bite. Munch, munch, munch. My fat, dumb dog. Fat, dumb, and sweet dog.

I should tell her to stop—my dog doesn't need the diabetes—but Priya's joy, her delight in this simple thing, charms me. Everything about Priya is so . . . I just want to . . . If I could only . . .

Shut. Up. Matty. Stop thinking about her. She believes she's not human.

And reminding myself of that makes me cool down—just a bit. I lean my head back outside the tent flap and feel the approach of the storm. The cool breeze slows my racing heart to a hundred miles an hour from a million; my blood lowers from a rolling boil to a simmer.

A droplet of rain plops onto my cheek. Then another and another until it's a steady sheet. I seal up the flap and shiver giddily despite the heat. I feel like a little kid, cozy in my tent with my dog and snacks, content and secure as if the thin nylon around me were an iron-clad barricade against intruders and not just a waterproof shell.

Hard to tell how long this storm will last. It's fast-moving, though; thunder cracks twice more like the sky is splitting, and Ginger tries to climb on top of Priya's lap. I resist the urge to pull her away. They seem so happy together.

"Did you do this as a kid, too?" I ask her. "Camp outside during storms?"

She thinks a moment, and her long fingers dig into the scruff around Ginger's neck. "No, this is not something we did. But I like it," she adds with a hint of a smile.

119

"Even though it means you can't get home tonight?"

She looks at me with pity in her brown eyes. "That is not what it means, Matthew. Rain will not deter my . . . what did you call it? Mother ship?"

"But . . ." I feel dumb. And sad. And yeah, disappointed. But mostly dumb. Rain doesn't stop planes from flying. Why would it stop a spaceship?

Spaceship? Did I just . . . ?

". . . unfortunately, no contact is possible."

I missed something. "Excuse me? What did you say?"

"Regardless of weather, the ship is on its way, but unfortunately no contact is possible." Priya peels a dried lump of cheese that has stuck to the cardboard box and feeds half to the dog, holding the other half in her fingers. "In the meantime I will continue to collect data."

I see Ginger eyeing the other piece of cheese. Cheese is one of my dog's most favorite things ever; the mere hint of it drives her into a frenzy. She's watching Priya's hands as they flutter in the air while she talks, her eyes on the prize.

". . . items I believe will be useful to my people . . ."

"Um, Priya?"

". . . flora and fauna of the area are unusual . . ."

"Priya? You might want to—"

And then it happens. Ginger lunges at Priya's hand and snatches the cheese from her fingers. Startled, Priya tries to scramble away, but with no place to go in this tiny tent, she falls over and lands directly on my thigh. I catch her before her bony elbow digs into my ribs.

"Oh!" Our eyes meet and she smiles, her chin to her chest. I see a blush bloom in her cheeks and wonder if the same is happening to me. It feels very warm in here.

"I'm sorry," I tell her. "I tried to warn you."

She pulls back, righting herself but sticking closer to me than to the dog. When she shakes her head, her white hair grazes my nose.

I want to trail my finger against her cheek, feel the down of her skin and the gentle slope of her cheekbone. If I wasn't blushing before, I must be now.

Well, it *is* a small tent.

"It's my fault," she says. "The dog was merely being a dog."

"That dog is more than a dog. That dog is, like, two dogs."

Priya giggles. "That doesn't make sense. How can one dog be like two?"

"Well, she's usually a good, sweet dog, but then she sees cheese and she's all . . ." I lunge at Priya's hand, grabbing her fingers in mine as if I were Ginger taking a chomp on them, which sends Priya into a gale of laughter.

"She's evil, you know? Good dog, evil dog. Two dogs in one."

Priya gently loosens her fingers from my grip but allows her hand to linger.

Or at least it feels that way to me.

"No, there is no good or evil. Not in a dog. Not in a person."

"No?"

"What is good to you may be evil to another person." She strokes the back of Ginger's head and my sweet, dumb dog continues to try to lick her hand, hoping for more food. "This dog wants cheese, which is good for her. But when she bites my fingers it's evil to me. Who is right?"

"You."

Priya's smile is quiet and small. For a moment all we hear is rain falling on the nylon tent. It's slowed some but remains steady. No stargazing tonight. I take my cell phone out and turn on the flashlight. It's almost too much light for this small tent, too intimidating. I tuck it beside the pizza boxes and the beam bounces off the nylon instead.

"Matthew, when I go, that will be good for me, yes?"

Don't say it.

"But it will be—"

"Ginger! Come here, girl. Want some cheese?" I know what Priya's trying to say and honestly, I just don't need to hear it spoken out loud. Maybe it will matter to me when she leaves and maybe it won't.

We'll just see when the time comes.

I feed the dog a big glob of mozzarella and try not to think.

Priya is quiet again, which makes me wonder what *she's* thinking. If I stare hard enough at her, can I read *her* mind?

Down at the house, Mom and Jack are probably still talking, still bitching about their loser spouses. I'll take the rain and the smell of wet dog over that any day. "So, Priya, listen . . ."

She cups her hand behind her ear. "Yes, Matthew. I have not shut off my hearing."

"Um . . . do you . . ." *Wanna hang out?* The memory of Emily's emphatic "no" is seared into my brain, and the thought that Priya would reject me too is frightening.

And yet . . . if I don't try and she leaves . . . will I forever wonder if this crazy-beautiful girl might have said yes?

"You wanna collect some data with me tomorrow? If you're here, I mean."

Priya's face lights up. It's as if I'm suddenly speaking her language. "Yes, if I am here, I would like that. As long as you promise me I'll be back to wait for my ride home."

"Absolutely." I feel a huge wave of relief wash over me, quickly followed by massive nausea. Now what?

"What data will we collect?"

"Oh, um, I don't know." I hadn't thought very far in advance. What do I do that's worth "collecting"? Riding motocross? Smoking weed? I'll think of something.

"You'll think of something," she says with a grin.

I poke my head out of the tent and feel the rain against my face. It's not a storm anymore, but it's still coming down pretty steady. "Are you going to be okay out here? You can stay at the house tonight. I can sneak you in."

"My ride—"

"Your ride. Right. Okay, well, you've got the rest of that pizza in case you get hungry again, and well, I guess I'll see you in the morning." *I hope.*

"Matthew, could you . . . ?" Her hand rubs her temple. "The pills you gave me. Do you have more?"

"Yeah, of course." I dig a finger into my jeans pocket and pull out the loose pills.

See, Mom? For once, it's a good thing I didn't put my clothes in the wash.

I roll all the pills into Priya's hand and curl her fingers around them. "If you need more, just come down."

When Ginger and I hike back, I find Mom alone at the kitchen table.

"Where have you been?"

"You noticed I was gone?"

"Not you. I'm talking to the dog." My mom's smile is tired. "Where's the pizza?"

"Oh, I, um . . ."

"You ate it all yourself?" She looks past me toward the field. Can she see Priya from here? I follow her gaze, but it's impossible to see anything beyond the willows.

I rub the dog's head. "Just me and Ginger. We were hungry."

My mother wobbles to her feet, swaying like one of the willow branches, her eyes half closed. She's buzzed—not completely wasted, but I wouldn't want to drive with her.

I follow her up the stairs, ready to catch her in case she stumbles, and she turns to me as we part at the second floor. "Matty, love . . ." She blinks slowly and moves her mouth, forming the words. "Love is . . . shit, it's complicated. You think it's gonna be easy when you fall in love. You think a kiss is forever and you'll be the center of their world." She aims a sloppy pointer finger at her chest. "I . . . your dad . . . we . . ."

I sigh and try not to roll my eyes. "You love him, I get it."

My mother lifts her chin; her nose is red, her cheeks pale under her freckles.

"No," she says harshly. And again: "No."

Her gaze finds me and nails me. I feel my breath behind my ribs, stuck in my lungs.

"I hate him. I hate him." And her eyes fill with tears.

2:47 A.M.

How can it still be raining? I take out my binoculars and find Priya in the tent. Without the moon and stars, it's incredibly dark out there. I should have left a flashlight or my phone. Is she scared?

I'm sure she's fine. She's been out there for three nights already, hasn't she? Nothing's happened so far, has it?

But. Rain.

She might . . . I don't know. Melt?

It doesn't matter, I just don't like her out there by herself.

I grab a blanket from a drawer in the guest room, find a pocket flashlight in the nightstand, and tiptoe down the back staircase. "Come on, Ginger girl," I coo at the sleepy

Lab, who's been enjoying the coziness of indoors. She's not going to like being outside, but that's just too bad. Maybe I can tempt her with the rest of the pizza I left with Priya.

We dash between the raindrops and I cautiously peel up the tent flap.

Priya is sound asleep with her arms wrapped around the telescope. I have to swallow hard to hold back a laugh. Damn, that's cute. I tuck the blanket around her waist and over her legs and hips, very carefully so I don't wake her. The flashlight I place next to her hand. Getting the dog inside, however, is not so simple. Eventually I have to wave some cheese in front of her nose. She hesitates but then follows it inside because, well, cheese.

I finally let her have it once she's in the tent. "Down, girl." She drops to the ground. "Stay, girl." She doesn't like it, but she's a good dog who passed her puppy exams years ago. She knows. She stays.

I lower the tent flap and hurry back to the house. I breathe.

But what if the ship comes and takes Ginger, too?

Can dogs live in outer space?

I honestly can't believe I just had that thought.

DAY FOUR

10:01 A.M.

Priya is outside the tent when I run up the hill. She tilts her head to one side and a sliver of sun catches the diamond stud in her nose. The sun is shining and the air is clear and I'm out of breath again, but this time it's not from running.

It's her. It's relief. It's . . .

Fine. It's all fine. "Hey. You still up for hanging out? Collecting some data?"

Priya's smile grows. "Yes! My . . . what is the word? Mentor?"

"You have a mentor?"

"Not mentor. Someone you . . . are responsible to?

You . . ." She shakes her head, suddenly impatient and frustrated.

"Work for?"

"Work? No. No," she repeats, biting off the word. "That is not what I mean."

"Well, maybe it will come to you."

She wrings her hands, clearly unsatisfied by my answer. Clearly upset she hasn't found the right word to describe her—

"Teacher?"

"Yes! Teacher. We are all teachers on my planet. We teach each other new things we have learned. I am a teacher." Happy again. *Whew.*

"Good. Maybe you can teach me some things." Did that just come out pervy? Honestly, I didn't mean it that way. Not entirely. "All right, let's get going. You have a lot of data to collect." We start down the small hill with Ginger, side by side by side. I'm not five feet away from her when Priya's knees buckle and she collapses to the ground. She doesn't even try to stop herself, though—her arms just hang by her sides as she drops to the grass. I hurry to help her up. Her eyes blink, bewildered by her body. "You okay?"

Her surprise turns to annoyance. "Yes."

"Maybe you just need some breakfast." I cup my palms under her elbows to steady her.

"Gravity," she says, nearly spitting the word. "Your planet's gravity is much stronger than ours. I told you," she adds, irritated. "My planet is much smaller and far less dense. The gravitational force is less. Moving—walking—everything is harder for me here."

"Okay, I just don't want you to fall again. That's not a bad thing, you know. To not want you to get hurt."

She brings a hand to the back of her head. "My pain . . . is back."

"You need more Tylenol?"

She shakes her head, wincing. "I'll be fine."

"Maybe we should stay—"

"No, no, I want to go," she says, grabbing my arm with both of her hands. The warmth of her touch radiates all the way to my scalp, upping my core temperature, and I immediately forget she just snapped at me. And then she takes my hand, squeezing it. I glance at it, at its smallness in mine, and then at her. She smiles shyly. "To help me? So I don't fall."

I find my voice. "Yeah, okay, sure." Very carefully, I lead her down the gentle slope, parting the weeping willow branches as if we were walking through a waterfall, and lifting her over the creek. She weighs about as much as my mom.

I lead her to the garage and realize I'll have to take my dirt bike if we want to go anywhere. Emphasis on the dirt part.

Then again, this is a girl who's been hanging out and sleeping and most likely peeing in a field. I hand her my helmet. "You have to wear this." My mom would kill me if I let her ride without one.

"Your mother would not be happy if I did not," she says.

How the hell does she do that?

I show her how to fasten it and then motion for her to hop on behind me. "You'll have to, um, hold my, um . . . here." I put my own hands on my waist like a moron. Jeez, you'd think I'd never been around a girl before. I mean, like, seriously, I want to tell myself to stop acting like she's a . . . an . . .

Alien?

She's just a girl. Just a pretty, clumsy girl who happens to think her lack of coordination is due to Earth's gravity.

Okay.

I feel her arms slide around my waist, feel her chest press against my back. Just two thin layers of cotton separate our naked bodies.

I feel a shiver up my spine. Oh my god, I'm five. Seriously, I'm five years old around Priya. When I glance over my shoulder at her, our noses touch. She giggles in my ear and nestles her chin at the back of my neck.

"Hold on." I rev the engine and tear out of the driveway.

You can probably visit every single thing in our town in half a day. Less than that. Three hours, tops. She's already seen the number-one thing on the Unofficial Visitors List: the space field. What's left after that?

Leaving our street, I have to drive past two miles of

farms before I get to what we call our town center. The road curves like a fat S and I feel Priya slide on the seat behind me. Her hands grip me tighter as she struggles to hold on. A shudder snakes through my body.

I swear I'm not swerving on purpose.

I have to slow down when we get to the main drag, such as it is. We have a few vigilant cops who have nothing better to do than nail people going a mile over the speed limit or who run the single stop light in front of the library. Plus this bike's not street legal. It's for off-roading only.

Whatever.

Oh, the library. That's a thing. As I idle at the light, I thrust a hand toward a brick building with a slate roof. "That's the library," I tell Priya, raising my voice so she can hear me.

"And that's the fire station." I point across the street where several volunteer firefighters are soaping up a truck. Soap bubbles escape, scattering on the wind, popping like pin-pricked balloons. We have a paramedic truck too, but that looks like it's out on business. Someone must have had a heart attack or something. Ate too much scrapple with their fried eggs.

The light turns and we get to the commercial block: the Dairy Queen and Dunkin' Donuts and pizza parlor.

And . . . we're done.

Ha. No, seriously. We're done. We have a junior-senior high school and an elementary school right next to each other. The schools even share a parking lot, which is more than a little embarrassing when a bunch of kids catch you smoking in your car. They tend to point and yell, "I'm tellin' your mom!"

I drive for another ten minutes, up and down the side streets, in some of the nicer neighborhoods as I search for something cool. I think of visiting my mom, but the hospital where she works is two towns over. I think of my uncle Jack, whose showroom has some high-tech cars, but he's two towns over in the opposite direction.

We have no pool, no movie theater, no Starbucks. Even the lake is just past the town line.

I suddenly realize I have nothing to show Priya. My town is boring as shit. We have absolutely zilcho here.

No wonder Em is going to Penn State.

No wonder my dad left.

I tool around the DQ and Double D for a second time, hoping something awesome will spontaneously occur. Maybe a fight will break out or a drunk guy will spill hot coffee all over himself. But while we watch, nothing happens. I stop the bike under the shade of a wide-leaved oak tree and flip the kickstand down. Priya stays on the bike, her arms still hugging me.

"I guess there isn't much to see."

I glance over my shoulder and see Priya's eyes light up. "I saw so much already!"

"You don't have to say that. I mean, you're being really nice, but—"

"Nice?" She cocks her head to one side as if defining the word for herself. "No. I'm not being nice."

"Please. A brick high school isn't exactly something to write about in your notebook," I say, aiming my chin at her bag.

As if in answer, she closes her eyes, head bobbing, whispering words in a language I don't understand.

Finally, she opens her eyes and holds my gaze. "I have felt the wind on my face in a new way. I have heard birds sing and smelled fresh soap. I have seen the beautiful homes of people I have never met. I have traveled miles on this . . ." She looks down at her lap.

"Dirt bike?" I suggest.

She nods. "Dirt bike. Which I have never done before." She takes off the helmet and shakes out her white-black hair. She tilts her chin up to the sky. "I am now enjoying the cool shade and delicate breeze of this tree. It is all more than I knew before." She slowly lowers her gaze to meet mine. "Your life is full of wonder, Matthew."

"It is? It sure as hell doesn't seem like it."

Priya slides off the bike and walks up to the tree, runs her hand along the bark. "This tree has so much to tell us."

"It's. A. Tree," I say slowly. "It can't talk."

Priya grins and rests her cheek against the trunk.

"Because it can't speak your language, you think it can't tell you anything? Listen to it."

I roll my eyes and cup my hand behind my ear. "Nope. I don't hear a word."

She reaches for me and pulls me by the hand to the tree. I fall into her and our faces are inches from each other. She places her ear against the bark and urges me to do the same.

I feel like an idiot. Thank god it's too early for most people to be buying Blizzards here at the DQ.

Priya closes her eyes again as if she truly is listening to the tree. I don't, because that's stupid. And because I don't need to have anyone watching me literally hug a tree.

"What do you—"

Priya clamps a hand over my mouth to quiet me. I taste dirt on my lips from where her fingers touch my mouth and I smell something sweet and salty. The pizza, I realize. It's from the pies we wolfed down last night.

"You want to know what I hear," she says. "I hear the ripple of leaves as the winds blow. I hear the creak of the branches. I hear the silence this tree lives in."

The silence? How do you hear silence? I want to laugh but she's so serious. "You don't hear anything, is what you mean."

She pats the side of my head, her eyes still closed. "Just listen to something besides your own voice."

"Ouch. Okay." I close my eyes and press my ear to the bark. The nubby ridges are softer than they appear and the edges tickle my skin. But I hear nothing. . . .

Wait. I hear . . . the wind blow across the bark like it's a musical instrument. I hear . . . the rustle of a squirrel running up the trunk. I hear . . .

. . . Priya's soft exhale.

As I open my eyes, she does too. A sudden gust of wind sweeps Priya's white hair across her face, making it cling to her eyelashes and the bark of the tree and my lips. I taste coconut. I doubt aliens use coconut shampoo.

She pulls her head away from the trunk and gently plucks strands of her hair from her eyelashes and the bark—and my lips. She laughs and I feel suddenly aware of being under a tree at the Dairy Queen with a girl who's giggling into her hair. I take her by the hand and lead her back to the bike.

Fastening the helmet over her head, she glances back wistfully at the tree, as if she were saying good-bye to an old friend she won't ever see again. Then her eyes meet mine and I see sadness shift to a glimmer of delight. "Will you take me on another adventure like this?"

"For real? This was just a stupid tree," I say, shaking my head. "And it's not even in, like, a forest or something cool. It's just, you know, a DQ."

"But this was data I didn't have and now I have it," she says. She taps her finger against the helmet. "It will all go back with me to my planet and everyone will benefit." Her smile is so genuine, so joyful, so contagious that I smile back. I don't want to, but fuck it, I do.

"Come on, space girl. Get on the damn bike." When she hugs my waist, I feel my stomach cinch; and when her chest presses against my back and her lips against my neck, I almost can't breathe.

3:52 P.M.

After I've shown her the rest of our town, including the park where Brian, Em, and I used to play on the swings, I circle back to my house. Ginger runs to the garage as soon as I pull in, barking and wagging her tail. She seems happier to see Priya than me.

I realize I'm starving and offer Priya a sandwich when we get to the kitchen. "Peanut butter and jelly?"

Holy shit, it's hot in here. Mom left the windows closed and the humidity formed like a fog, settling smack in the kitchen. I kick the door open and try to let the air circulate, but the heat is insane.

Looking over my shoulder, Priya wrinkles her nose

when I open the jar of peanut butter. It's the crunchy kind that Mom loves. "I don't think I'll like this," she says.

"No? What about this?" I open the jelly. It's grape.

She sniffs deeply and smiles. "I think I'll like this instead."

"Of course. It's all sugar." I pull down a loaf of wheat bread and get out plates and glasses. Ginger is so excited to have a guest in the house that she's hopping and jumping from me to Priya, from the table to the door to the fridge. Always hoping for a pat on the head or an extra snack. I lean into the fridge to search out sodas. Turning my head, I ask, "Priya, do you want something to—"

"Oh!" she says, suddenly collapsing on one side. I watch as her left arm and left leg buckle like a deflating balloon. As before, she doesn't even try to stop herself with her arms but drops straight to the stone floor. Ginger and I both rush to her and grab her before her head can hit the ground.

"Priya!" Her head bobbles on her neck and her chest rises and falls quickly as she tries to catch her breath. I cradle her in my arms on the floor, afraid to move her. Her eyelashes flutter and her limbs go rigid with fright, but when her wide eyes find mine, she relaxes against me. "You need help," I tell her. "Professional, medical help."

"No!"

"Priya, I have to—"

"Please, no. Please."

"But—"

"No. No. It's . . . it's gravity," she mumbles. "Very vexing. Very challenging."

I want to call her on the bullshit but instead I laugh. I have to. I'm so relieved she didn't hurt herself. She's so stubborn, but at least she's not injured. Not that I can see, anyway. "Maybe you need to get out of the heat."

"If you can't stand the heat, get out of the kitchen," she says with a perfectly straight face.

"Where did you hear that?" I help her up, allow her to test her weight against me, and then guide her to a chair at the wooden table. Ginger's tail swishes against her legs and she rests her giant head on Priya's lap.

"I've collected a lot of data, Matthew," she says. "Some of it will be useful. But not all of it."

I spread a thick layer of purple jam on one slice of bread, add a layer of unsalted butter on the other slice, and then press them together to mush the flavors in. This is a sandwich my dad used to like. No peanut butter for him, either, because he's allergic to nuts. I cut the sandwich into two triangles and arrange them on a plate.

"So what other data have you collected?" I ask her as I set the plate in front of her and go back to make my own sandwich. Extra peanut butter. Extra jelly. Maybe even a double-decker with an extra slice of bread.

"Everything I see, I collect," she says simply.

"Everything?"

"*Every*thing." When I catch her eye, I swear she's

winking slyly at me. She takes a bite of her sandwich and chews thoughtfully.

"What do you think?"

"It's not as flavorful as the pizza."

"Hell no. Pizza is the best food on the planet."

"Maybe on *your* planet," she says. Oh yeah, that was a sly nod in my direction.

"And on yours? What's the best food?"

She shakes her head. "I told you, we don't eat like you do. You wouldn't understand."

"Try me." I take my sandwich and sit across from her. She's already eaten half the sandwich, I notice. Do they have grape jelly and butter on her planet?

She settles back in the chair and her hands wander to Ginger's giant head. She strokes the dog's soft ears absentmindedly as a thoughtful look crosses her face. "Our meals are communal. We share food just as we share our thoughts."

"Okay. Family style. Big bowls of food, I got it."

"It's not just the food and family. It's the shared community that makes a meal," she says urgently. "What you call family is not what we call family."

I stuff half the sandwich into my mouth at once and swallow it with some Coke. "You don't have parents? No brothers or sisters?"

"We do, strictly speaking, but we're raised by the community." She opens her arms into a circle and then gathers the space between them like she's hugging the air.

"Yeah, okay, so . . . what do you eat?"

She laughs. "*That's* what you want to know?"

I polish off the sandwich and get up to make another. "Pretty much. I mean, I get the whole 'it takes a village' crap. That's nothing new. And I understand people having conversations at the dinner table." She opens her mouth to speak and I hold up my peanut butter knife to stop her. "I know. You don't actually *talk*. You think at each other. Whatever. I'm pretty sure I saw that in an episode of *Star Trek*." I slap some jelly on another slice of wheat bread. It's too much, though, and squirts out the sides when I press the slices together.

Ginger is immediately at my feet, as if she could hear the PB&J squishing on my plate. I take the sandwich off and set the plate down for her to clean up.

"Do you have parents?" Priya asks me.

"Yep."

"Do you have any brothers or sisters?"

Brian is kind of like my brother, although Em is hardly a sister. That would be fucked up for sure. Like *Game of Thrones* fucked up. "No. But it's okay. I like being an only child."

"Are you lonely?"

I hesitate. For most of my life, I was never lonely. I had my dad and we did everything together. Brian and I might have ridden our bikes every day after school, but it was my dad who taught me how to ride. Brian and I watched marathons of *Star Trek*, but it was my dad who introduced me to the show. I know about stars and planets and history because of my dad. For a very long time, we were best buds.

I shake my head. "I've got two good friends. Brian and Emily. They're the best. You'll meet them."

Her smile is wistful. "Perhaps."

"Oh right, you'll be gone soon." I don't believe those words. Truly, I don't. She's not getting a lift to the sky at any point in my lifetime. It just ain't gonna happen. But *she* believes it and that belief sinks into my stomach like a stone. "Well, you'll just have to leave us your email and we'll Skype with you." I grin to show her I'm not completely serious, although I kind of am. Who knows?

I feel sweat trickle down my back and face and into the itchy five-o'clock shadow I get by midafternoon.

Midafternoon! *Oh crap.* I grab Priya's hand and pull her out the door. "We have to get to Brian's. Gotta feed Boo." She looks at me quizzically. "More data collection."

4:47 P.M.

I've opened all the doors and windows again, letting the fresh air blow out the cat smells and the humidity. I have no idea where Boo is, but I'm sure she'll come slinking out as soon as I open the fridge.

Priya wanders around the kitchen while I run cool water from the tap for the cat and clean out the food bowl. Over my shoulder I can see her studying photographs of Brian and Em with their parents, a happy foursome on vacation at Hersheypark and the Jersey Shore and Gettysburg. Were my parents ever that happy?

"Did you take vacations like that when you were a kid?" I ask her.

Priya runs a finger along a photo of the Aokis posing with the Phillies mascot, the tall green long-snouted Phanatic.

"Vacations? I have never been on a vacation," she says.

"Really? No trips to the Grand Canyon or Yosemite?" I wipe out Boo's water bowl before refilling it. Water is not enough to draw her from wherever she's hiding.

She shakes her head. "Would these be for data collection?"

"Uh, yeah, if you're collecting fun." I take out the veggies and chicken, chop them, and blend them as I did yesterday. Like magic, Boo appears at my feet, wrapping herself around my legs in a figure eight.

"Felicette!" Priya cries. As her outstretched arms reach for Boo, the cat suddenly notices the back door is open and bolts for it.

"Wait! Boo! No!"

Priya looks stricken. "Felicette?"

I drop the food on the counter and hurry into the backyard, but I don't see the cat anywhere. "Shit. She's gone. Emily's gonna kill me."

"Your friend will kill you?" Priya is horrified.

"Quite possibly yes, if anything happens to that cat."

"Felicette will be fine. She's a brave cat."

I turn to Priya, who is following me on her tiptoes through the long grass of the backyard. "Who is Felicette? This is Boo."

For a moment, Priya looks confused, and then she shakes her head with a light laugh. "Yes, yes, I know. Felicette was the first cat in outer space. She was trained by the French and sent up in a research rocket in the year you designated as 1963."

"Nineteen sixty-three? That cat is long gone by now." I wonder how far the Aokis' property goes. Could Boo have run to a neighbor's house? To the street? To the DQ? "Boo is not an outdoor cat," I say. "She's been inside her whole life. Emily never lets her out."

Behind me, Priya steps delicately as if she were avoiding treading on individual blades of grass. "Felicette parachuted back to Earth," she tells me. "I wonder what she thought as she was floating."

"Get me down!" I say in a high-pitched voice.

"I think she enjoyed it. If you were a cat, wouldn't you like to fly?"

"I guess. It would certainly make it easier to chase birds."

We're at the edge of the Aokis' yard. Beyond this are dense woods. If Boo is in here, it will be nearly impossible to find her. I can feel myself sigh. Only two days into their vacation and I'm going to have to tell Emily I lost her cat.

I feel Priya's hand on my shoulder. Her fingers press into my back and rest there. "This sucks," I tell her. "Emily already hated me. Now she'll never speak to me again."

"She doesn't hate you. She would not ask someone

she hates to watch her cat."

"You don't know Em."

"I don't know Em, but that behavior would not make sense."

"Boo! Where are you? Boo!"

"You are doing this wrong. She will not come to you."

"How do you know? Boo! Come here, Boo!" But I know she's right. Boo isn't a dog; she's not like Ginger, who responds the exact same way all the time. I know that when I clap my hands and whistle, Ginger will come to me. I know that if I shake a box of biscuits, she'll sit up and beg. I know that she loves to chase balls and birds and that she barks when she's excited. I know what to expect from her every single day. And I like that. I don't like . . . change. I don't like . . . unpredictability. I don't like . . . risks.

Asking Emily out was a no-brainer. I mean, we'd known each other for years. We hooked up. She knew I crushed on her—she *knew*. Didn't she? It shouldn't have been a risk at all. It should have been an easy "yes."

I feel Priya's hand slide down my back and her fingers intertwine with mine. Why exactly am I thinking about Emily?

She gently tugs me back toward the house.

"But Boo—"

"The cat is not out here."

Even as I allow her to lead me through the yard, I shake my head. "How do you know that?"

Priya taps her finger at her temple. "Because I am thinking like a cat. That's what you must do."

"Think like a cat? You mean, *Oh boy, I'm gonna climb this tree and eat that mouse?*"

"Your cat has been inside for all of her life, yes?"

"Yes."

"Then why would she run away?"

"Because it's new and different? I don't know. I'm not a cat."

Priya touches the side of my face now. "Think like a cat."

We're back at the house and the door is still wide open, but there is no sign of Boo. "I'm telling you, she's gone."

Priya positions herself at the back door and looks right, then left, then right again. Still holding my hand, she pulls me along the side of the house, past the cellar stairs and the grill, over the stone patio, and around the table and chairs.

We get to the side porch and Priya pauses by the stairs. "Think like a cat," she says again, and drops to her knees. She ducks her head under the stairs and I hear a muffled "Aha!"

I follow her gaze to a pair of glow-in-the-dark eyes peeking at us from the other end of the deck. There is barely enough room for my head and shoulders under here; no way could I crawl to the cat to get her out. "Boo!"

Priya's fingers pinch my wrist. "Do not scare her."

"But how will we—"

"We wait. We keep thinking."

We crawl out from under the porch and sit in reverent silence, but as the minutes tick by, Boo makes no move to come out.

"Are you sure that's a cat and not a raccoon?"

Priya smiles slyly at me. "We are now just waiting for Felicette's parachute to open and for her to float back to Earth."

I grin and feel relief spread through my body. "How did you know she was going to be under the porch and not a mile from here?"

"She doesn't want to run away."

"Did you mind-meld with the cat?"

"Mind-meld?"

"It's a Vulcan thing. Forget it."

"Yes, I know about Vulcans." Her fingers squeeze mine. "You're teasing me."

"I am."

"I don't mind."

"Good, because I don't plan to stop." Our eyes meet and I try to send her a message. *If you can read my mind, please don't go. Please stay.*

"If you were a cat who had lived its whole life inside and you finally got a chance to go outside, you would not be grateful, you would be terrified," Priya says. "Indoors is safety and security and food and love. It is your home. The outdoors is not your home."

I feel her leg against mine, her arm against mine, her

shoulder and hip pressed into me very subtly, very gently, as if we are relaxing into each other, melting into each other.

"We all just want to be home, don't we?" she says without looking at me.

Where is your home? Where is your family? I want to ask but Priya gasps and sits up sharply.

"Felicette! You have returned to Earth." Boo, covered in dirt and cobwebs, climbs on top of Priya's lap and begins to lick her paws clean.

"Thank god." I start to take the cat from Priya but Boo holds fast, her nails digging into the fluffy layers of skirt. "Okay, okay, stay with her, I don't care. I don't even like cats."

I give Priya a hand as she clutches Boo and tries to stand up. Her wide eyes blink slowly. "You are more like this cat than you think," she says.

What does that *mean?* I wonder.

8:39 P.M.

It's been forever since I've set this thing up, since my dad and I were side by side, each of us capturing a quadrant of the sky in our sights. Even so, my fingers know exactly where to go. Without a glance down, I unscrew the tripod legs and level it in a heartbeat, no second-guessing.

My Celestron has an equatorial mount, which means it's easy to track objects across the sky but more complex to use because there are two gears to unlock and adjust, the right ascension and the declination. You unlock the gears, swivel it close to your target, then use the fine-tuning knobs to center it in your finderscope.

"Libra?" I ask Priya. "Is that what we're looking for?"

"Yes," she says with a tilt of her head. I can feel her impatience. Ever since we came back from Brian's, she's been bugging me to set up the telescope. Finally it's dark enough.

"You're sure it's Libra, huh? It's not Cassiopeia or something else?" I tease her, although maybe, just maybe, it's a test. How committed to this is she, really?

"Matthew, my planet is not in another constellation. It is in what you call Libra."

"Yeah, yeah. I'm just joking."

I glance up at the sky to orient myself and find the Big and Little Dippers with my naked eye. Then I look through the scope, sighting the same thing. Libra is a summer constellation for stargazers in the northern hemisphere; a triangle of stars forms the scales. To find it, first you face south and locate the bright red star Antares in Scorpius. If you follow the line of stars that forms the scorpion's body to the right, the next-brightest stars are Zubeneschamali and Zubenelgenubi in Libra.

Stardust swirls in front of my eye and I feel my breath inhale sharply. It's as if I've been instantly transported back in time, back to the very first time my dad showed me how to find things in our vast Universe.

"Check it out, Junior. Those dots of light are all stars, billions and billions of stars," he said, his voice hushed as if anything louder than a whisper would blow them all away.

"But where's the moon?" I remember asking. "Is it gone?"

He laughed. "It's there but we can't see it now." He added, "And if it *were* there, we wouldn't be able to see much at all. The light would block out everything else." He was so happy to teach me what he knew. And when I was five, he knew *everything*.

I find Antares but it's too far away, so I swap out the eyepiece and refocus, and the sky explodes with stars. My breath catches in my throat; it feels like I've just dived into a pool of starlight.

I feel Priya and Ginger behind me, both within arm's reach.

"Libra is an okay constellation but kind of boring."

"Boring?" Priya asks. "Stars do not have a personality."

"Sure they do. I think there are lots more interesting constellations," I say. "Like Cassiopeia."

I feel Priya's hands wave the air impatiently. "Your preference for constellations is unimportant."

"You know the story of Cassiopeia, don't you . . . Ginger?" I say, turning to my dog. "Cassiopeia was an Ethiopian queen who thought she was more beautiful than any of the Nereids, the sea nymphs. The god of the sea, Poseidon, got angry at her arrogance and demanded she sacrifice her daughter, Andromeda. Cassiopeia's husband, the king, chained Andromeda to a rock and then Poseidon sent a sea monster to eat her."

Priya gasps, which makes me smile. I do some further fine-tuning and fill the scope with more and more of the star field.

"Andromeda was very beautiful. Perseus offered to rescue her if he could marry her. Her parents agreed and she was saved." I look at the dog again. "That's a good ending, don't you think, Ginger?"

I hear Priya mumble something behind me.

"Excuse me?"

"That is not the ending of the story," Priya says, coming closer to the telescope. "Poseidon wanted to humiliate Cassiopeia one final time for her hubris, so he placed her among the stars with her throne upside down. Half of every night, she hangs her head in shame."

I glance over my shoulder to Priya, who is now within a foot of me. I step back and allow her to look through the eyepiece, to find the planet she has been so eager and so desperate to see. "You know the story?"

"I gathered that data earlier in my visit," she tells me while she is bent down, both hands behind her back. Her stance tells me she's done this before. The true amateur astronomer knows to avoid touching the scope once it's in place; you don't want to bump it and have to reset. "But of course we have no such myth ourselves. We don't anthropomorphize the Universe."

She steps back from the telescope. "Will you increase the magnification for me, please?"

She also knows you never change the settings on a scope that isn't yours. Someone, somewhere, taught her manners about stargazing.

I make the adjustment and let her return to the scope. But I don't give her much room, so she has to squeeze her tiny frame between me and the telescope. Her body fits *so* perfectly. . . .

"May I adjust this?"

At first I think she's talking about something *else* but then I realize she means the telescope. "Yeah sure."

"Thank you." She makes the adjustments with one hand, like a pro. A moment later, I see her smile.

"There it is," she says breathlessly. "My planet."

I'm not sure what I expected to happen, but finding "her" planet was not one of them. I guess I was anticipating a frowny face and Priya's defensive insistence that my telescope was not powerful enough or that it was too far to see from here or some other bullshit, but actually finding something? "No . . . really?"

"Yes, really. I don't understand your incredulity."

"I believe you."

"No, you don't. You remain skeptical. Look."

I lean over her—she doesn't give *me* much room either, I notice—and peer through the eyepiece. She has focused the crosshairs on a speck that looks a shade brighter perhaps than the other stars in the sky. It's got a slight reddish-orange tint to it, which could be the star's distance from

Earth or its temperature or even how our eyes see things at night. It's impossible to know if that is a star or a dot of star-dust, a planet with life or a dead rock hurtling through space.

"I live there," she says in my ear. Her voice trembles with excitement.

"Priya—"

"You don't know if that's really a planet, right? Is that what you're thinking?"

Sigh. "Yes."

"You want to tell me that it's impossible to get from there to here."

"Yeah."

"And I'm telling you it isn't."

"But—"

"Why is your truth more accurate than mine? Why are you quick to dismiss my words as false?" Her tone is subtle, not accusatory, but I can tell she feels more confident than before. Finding the telescope, the constellation, the planet—have boosted her spirits.

"Your father would believe me."

I keep my eye on the orange spot, as if squinting hard enough might make me see a thousand tiny hands waving at me across the galaxy. "And how would you know that?"

"The star charts are your father's," she says quietly. "In the workshop. He believes there is more to the Universe than this planet. He believes this field is special."

Special. Startled, I back away from the telescope and

bump into Priya. Turning, I find her face gazing up at me. The blanket of stars lights up her eyes and her lips and the ends of her hair. "He believes, yeah. But he changed. He . . ." I scowl and look away. "He's an idiot."

"Why? Because he believes something you don't?"

I start to move away from Priya, but her long fingers grip my forearm and hold me fast. "Believes what? That a spaceship landed in this field? That he knows more than other people because something might have crashed at the moment he was born?" I lean into her. "Does that even make sense to you?"

Instead of answering me, she asks, "Are you sure you didn't believe it once too?"

"I . . . no. I . . . no, I never did." I shake my head from side to side. How could I have believed that crap? Galaxies and meteors and comets—I could *see* those. I knew they were real. But the other stuff? The alien autopsy shit and the crazy conspiracies? No, I never believed those. And I don't think he ever did either. They just suited his needs.

"You will never have proof. You have to have faith," says Priya.

Words my dad spoke years ago pop into my head: *"Absence of evidence is not evidence of absence."* When I was seven, nine, twelve, I trusted in those words. I didn't truly know what they meant, but if my dad said them, well, that was enough.

But words are not enough. Not anymore.

He lied to me, lied to my mom. He betrayed us both in big ways and small. He was selfish and wanted to be special, but he was just an ordinary man who had ordinary desires. After I discovered my dad's blog had become a forum for the conspiracy nuts, I asked him about it. I wanted to know why he hadn't told me or Mom.

We were in his workshop at the time, snow softly piling up outside, the wood-burning stove keeping us toasty. He stopped typing on his computer and his face reddened. "Oh well, your mom doesn't like it much. She thinks it's kind of out there," he said. "But you know what? A lot of people love it. Like, a ton." He shook his head with a look of wonder on his face. "They're, like, my followers."

"You mean they follow your blog?" When he nodded, I asked, "Does Mom know?"

He shrugged and went back to his computer. "She doesn't have time for that. Work and farm, remember? That's all she has time for these days. Work and farm."

"But what about me?" I asked him. "You could have told me."

I saw his back heave with a sigh. "You don't have time for me either." He turned his head toward me. "It's okay, Junior. You've got other things to do now."

I left feeling bad, feeling like I'd lost something, and I thought maybe I could get back to the astronomy with Dad. Maybe it would help him be a normal guy again.

But then this thing happened six months later. This

thing where I walked into my parents' bathroom looking for Q-tips I could use to clean the lens of my telescope and the water was running in the shower.

I knew Dad was home because I'd seen his truck.

I opened the door, calling to my dad, "Just me, looking for—"

And the woman in the shower who was not my mom poked her head around the curtain at that moment and said, "DJ, would you hand me—"

Her eyes were hazel and she was a blonde, her curly hair slick against her neck and shoulders. Her pink lips formed a little O when she saw me and she quickly ducked back into the shower without another word.

I grabbed the box of Q-tips and left, closing the door behind me, trying to get my pounding heart under control. *What the fuck?* I met my dad in the hallway. I took one look at him and all that confusion was replaced with disappointment.

How could he?

I pivoted and aimed myself down the hall. I needed to be anywhere but outside that bathroom at that moment.

"Junior, now wait," he said, grabbing me and holding me in place. "It's not what you think."

I stared at him. We were eye to eye for the first time ever. I guess I'd finished that last bit of growth spurt right about then.

"She's a follower," he said. "One of my followers." He

was proud of this. He sounded like he was the leader of a cult or something.

"Your *blog* followers?"

"Yes."

"What about Mom?"

"This has nothing to do with your mother."

"I think it kind of does."

He held me firmly. "It doesn't. And it won't be any good for her to know."

My mind reeled when I thought of my mom.

"You have to keep this to yourself," he said to me. "It's better that way."

"You can't do this again," I told him. "You can't have this woman over again."

He looked like he was considering it. Then he shook his head. "No, not again."

"Dad, I mean ever. Any of your damn followers. You can't . . . *have sex with them.*"

My dad's gaze narrowed at me, as if I were being so naive. "Junior, you can't—"

"No! You can't do this to Mom." My voice rose higher and higher, nearly to a squeak. "If you do, I swear I'll tell her! I'll tell her everything!"

"No, you won't."

"Yes! I will tell her. And I don't care if it hurts her. I want her to know the truth."

Mention of the truth always struck a chord with my

father. He was a truth seeker himself. After what seemed like an eternity, he nodded calmly, as if to himself, and said, "All right."

"You promise?"

"I promise." No hesitation, no furtive glance. He promised and I left him, relieved.

I never told my mother about it. Until three days ago when he left with Carol, I thought that was the end of his cheating.

I wanted to believe.

Priya squeezes my hand, calling me back to the present. Her gaze holds mine. "I'm real."

"True."

"You believe in me."

"I believe you are . . ." *Intelligent and charming.* "A nice human girl who might be . . ." *Nutty.* "A little misguided."

"Is that what you believe?" Her lips twitch provocatively, and suddenly I believe she really can read my mind. I know she can. The truth isn't *out there*; it's in here. It's in my face and in my voice and in the skin that she's touching.

I bend my face to hers, curve my shoulders around her, enveloping her, consuming her. I feel a wave of heat roll toward me from her very core, from her heart and her lungs. One hand slides along my arm and up to my shoulder, the other wraps around my waist. Her fingers twist my shirt into knots at my back.

We melt into each other, magnetized from waist to hips to thighs.

My eyes squeeze shut as our lips meet, and it would be crazy to say I see stars, wouldn't it?

So I won't say it.

But I feel it.

This is real. Her tongue against mine is real. Her back beneath my hands is real. Her legs entwined with mine . . .

Breathless, she pulls back and a breeze cools us down as we separate. But she doesn't let go. Her fingers cling to my shirt, damp from the humid air, from *us*. She looks up at me in surprise, bewildered. But how can that be? This can't be her first rodeo. She obviously knows what she's doing. That kiss, that passion? Oh-so-human.

"Priya?"

She blinks a few times and she looks around her, at the field, at me, as if she were finding something in her scope. When she gets me between her crosshairs, she grins. "Yes. That was . . ."

Awesome. "Nice."

"Yes. You call it . . . ?" Her head tilts and her white-black hair hangs to one side.

"Um . . . kissing?" All those times I wanted to touch her hair but stopped myself. I don't stop this time. My fingers caress the ends of her wig; the impossibly silky hairs don't clump together like normal hair. I feel like I'm touching a ghost's hair, smoothly ethereal.

"Kissing," she murmurs. "Kiss. Again."

I crush her to me. She responds with equal pressure,

hugging me to her chest, squeezing her arms around my neck. I let my lips wander to her ear and trail down to her shoulder.

A shiver runs up my spine when she does the same. It's as if she's echoing me. I kiss; she kisses. I touch; she touches. I taste; she tastes. . . .

Is this real? Like, really real? We're standing in a field, clutching each other as if there is no tomorrow, and maybe there won't be, not if she leaves—not by spaceship, not through a wormhole, but in a car or a bus or on foot.

No. I won't let her go. I'm not ready.

I pull her with me to the ground and lower her head gently against her bag. I line my body up with hers and let our legs tangle. Her tutu tickles my arm when I run my hand up the back of her leg and along the curve of her hips.

She's not like Emily. She doesn't have the muscular back and thighs that Em has. I can feel each vertebra in her spine as if it were a bulb on a string of Christmas lights.

I touch here, squeeze there, lick this, nibble that.

And she does the exact same to me.

I think she's going to stop me, that she's going to do what other girls have done and whisper, "No, not that," or "That's far enough."

She doesn't.

But we have to stop. We can't. Not here. Not in a field. Not with my dog watching. Well, maybe Ginger isn't watching, but she's here and that's just weird.

I hold back and take a deep breath so Priya will too. Gradually the pulse of my heart slows to the speed of a freight train.

Priya grins and brushes her hair away from her temples. "Thank you."

"Thank . . . me? Why?"

She taps the side of her head. "Data collection."

I laugh. I can't help it. "Right, yeah, okay. You're welcome."

"You taught me well."

"And now you'll teach others?"

She shakes her head. "I won't have to. They will know it because I know it."

"And what do you know?"

She answers me with the longest, deepest kiss I have ever experienced.

You have to stop. Now.

"Why do I have to stop?" she asks, in complete innocence. She has absolutely no idea what she's doing to me.

But it's my own fault. I started it.

Thank you, Matty.

You're very welcome, Matty.

I roll onto my back and look up at the stars. Beside me I feel Priya do the same. She stretches her legs straight in front of her like she always does and rests her arms on top of her thighs.

"I'll probably be leaving tonight," she says.

My heart knocks against my ribs. "What?"

"It's been three days since I anticipated my ship's arrival. My calculations aren't *that* wrong. They will be here very soon." Her tone is matter-of-fact, as if she and I didn't just make out like rabbits.

"Are you . . . are you sure?"

She reaches behind her and takes her notebook out of her bag. Holding it above her face, she tilts it so it catches the starlight. Flipping page after page, she makes little *hmmm* noises. Try as I might, I can't see what's on those pages. They could be grocery lists, for all I know. A celestial to-do that only she understands. Finally, she closes the book and places it back in her bag.

"I believe so," she says.

"Can I . . . stay here with you? Until you leave, I mean?"

She nods. "You can't come with me."

"I know," I say abruptly, and maybe a little too sharply. "I just want to see the ship and you know, wave good-bye."

"Wave?"

I hold my hand up and wave it in the air. Priya holds hers up too, matching it; we wave together, fingers pressed like bodies.

I have to stop thinking about her, about this. She's right. She's leaving. I have to accept that.

I lower our hands to the ground, let her fingers rest in my palm.

Don't go.

DAY FIVE

10:28 A.M.

By the time the sun warms my face, it's too late. I fell asleep
beside Priya and didn't go back to the house to tell Mom I
was home.

Priya is still on the ground, still flat on her back with
her feet pointed and her arms by her sides. Ginger must
have trotted over to her after I fell asleep, because her head
is nestled against the crook of my dog's neck, using her like
a furry pillow.

Damn dog didn't give *me* a place to rest my head.

I didn't *really* think a spaceship was going to pick up
Priya last night, but it is a relief to see her here. While
she sleeps, I stare at her, memorizing her for that moment

when she does eventually leave the field. In the sunlight, her skin appears bronze against my dog's dingy white coat and her hair shines like it was painted. I brush a lock of white from her face and feel the impossibly silky texture slip between my fingers. With her dimpled chin tilted up to the sky, her delicate neck exposed and vulnerable, she looks almost regal, like a princess, with her fluffy tutu and patent-leather boots.

"Is that it, Priya?" I whisper. "Are you royalty?" Not from another planet but somewhere here on Earth, in a small country on a tiny tropical island floating in the southern hemisphere? Or maybe she's a queen in exile, spirited away by courtiers while a coup takes place? Perhaps she doesn't even know she's the daughter of a deposed king. She doesn't even know she's special.

Someone must be missing her. A mother, a father, a younger sister who idolizes her.

A boyfriend?

I consider waiting with her until she wakes up, but I've got to check in with Mom before she flips out.

Or has she already?

Cop car in the driveway. Jack's Mustang right behind it. *Seriously, dude?*

I pause a few feet from the kitchen. Part of me wants to flee, to run back to Priya and grab her hand and just keep going. The part that wants to deal with my mom right now is infinitesimally small.

I circle around the front of the house to see if the entire police department is here, but there's just the single squad car—white with brown and yellow lettering, "Sheriff's Department" written on the side with a gold shield and the name of the county.

I clear my throat, readying myself to face Mom and the cop who came to investigate. He's one of the older guys, doesn't move so fast, wouldn't fare well in a shootout. Not that we get much of those around here. Round-faced, round-bellied, wearing a tan polyester jacket that's too heavy for this weather and too short for his bulk, he stands with his sweaty back to me, facing my mom and Jack in the hallway. Mom's face is tense with worry and fear and for a second, I feel a pang of guilt clench my stomach.

". . . your son has any friends he might be with?" he's saying as I step into the foyer.

My mother sees me and pushes the cop aside; relief replaces worry. "Matthew, where the hell have you been?" She's in her pj's and Jack's in his suit, which means she didn't flip out until this morning when she got up and I wasn't making coffee for her.

She grabs me by the sleeves and hugs me hard. My uncle pats me on the back as if I were the fine leather interior of a brand-new muscle car.

"Jeez, kid, you scared us," he says.

The cop jerks his thumb toward me, says to my mom, "This him?"

Your powers of deduction astonish me, Mr. Policeman. She nods and thanks him profusely for coming out and taking the time and she's very sorry, she hopes he wasn't called from something more important, thank you and good-bye and . . .

"Where were you, Matty?" she shouts as soon as the door closes. "You should know better than this."

"What?" is all I can manage. I mean, what am I supposed to say? The truth? I slept next to a crazy girl in an empty field while we waited for her spaceship to arrive?

"Did you make coffee?" I start for the kitchen, but my mother's gaze hardens and she crosses her arms over her chest as she paces in front of me, blocking my path.

"Answer me. Where were you?"

"I was around. Jeez. I was actually really, really close by," I say with a grin. "You could have called my name and I'd have come."

"I called your phone."

"Oh. Huh."

"Where. Were. You."

"I was . . ." My brain is in low gear, turning so slowly.

"Were you drinking? Smoking?"

"No! Don't you trust me?" I shake my head and walk past her and Jack. I need coffee. The pot is half empty. I pour myself a mug and hear flip-flops slap against the stone floor. I stare into my cup and shake my head. This is absurd, her calling me out like this.

"Face facts, Matty, you're starting to act just like your father," Mom says.

I take a gulp of hot coffee and scald my throat. "Seriously? You did *not* just say that to me." I glance over at Jack to see if he's on board with this. He catches my eye and then sheepishly stares at the creases in his fancy pants. Really? No love from the only other guy in the room? Thanks, man.

"I'm *not* like Dad, okay? I am nothing like him." I slosh the coffee around in the mug, cooling it off before I swallow the rest in two long gulps. I can't believe she would even say that to me. After all we've been through? I mean, I'm here every single day. I do what she wants. I make her coffee. I take care of the dog. Yeah, I smoke a little weed and maybe I could get better grades but I'm not a *cheater*. I don't *lie* to people and I don't betray their trust.

I slam the mug on the counter a little harder than I intend. I'm pissed but not break-a-cup pissed. "Maybe you need to go to work and stab someone with a needle or something."

"What?"

I probably just put a toe over the line, but why the hell stop there? Let's go for the whole two feet. "Take your bullshit frustrations out on some other chump. Not me."

My mother's face pales with anger and her freckles stand out like spots on a leopard. A very pissed-off leopard. "That is *not* the tone to take with me this morning," she says, her voice so low it sounds like a growl.

Again, I seek out Uncle Jack for support, for someone to agree that my mom is flipping out for no good reason, but he's got far more important things on his mind, like picking stray hairs off his jacket lapels.

"You know, I've got crap to do, so—"

"I think you should stay home and clean the house," Mom says. "Top to bottom, including both bathrooms."

"What? No." I've got a day with Priya ahead and there's no way in hell I'm spending it indoors.

"I am your mother—"

"And you're being completely unreasonable," I say. I don't like the sudden sweat that pours from my pits and the way my hands tremble. I shove them into my pockets. I swear I'll scream if she says something like . . .

"Go to your room."

I don't scream. I laugh. I tilt my head back and howl like an idiot. No way did she just say that. Hot tears spring to my eyes and I blink them back.

Now—*now*—my uncle steps in. "Lorna, do you really think that's necessary?" He smiles at me. "Matty's okay and nothing happened—"

"Jack, shut up, please. When you have kids, you can do things your own way."

Since when has my mother done things *this* way? Since when has she kept a leash around my neck? Since when has she thought the worst of me?

Since Dad left her.

Jack and I both realize this at once and try to talk sense into Mom.

"He's seventeen, Lorna, not a child—"

"Mom, come on, I'm—"

"I'm not going to stand here and argue," she says, looking up at each of us. She's so tiny; she's like an ant putting her foot down in front of two giraffes. "I have to go to work." She throws a glance at Jack. "And you do too."

My uncle starts to say something. Maybe something along the lines of "You don't control me" or "I'm glad you're not *my* wife"? But he just shakes his head instead and lifts his hand in a wave as he heads out the front door. "See ya later, Lorna." He calls over his shoulder to me, "Glad you're safe, Matty."

My mother stomps around the kitchen in her plastic shoes and makes a big show of getting her travel mug without my help. No sir, she doesn't need my assistance. She can just reach up there on her toes and use her fingertips to ease a thermal carafe off the shelf and voilà, done. She doesn't need me, doesn't need Dad. Nope.

The silence in the kitchen is like an invisible entity, its presence sucking the air out of the room. I feel the weight of a thousand unspoken words crushing me. I want to be kind, to tell my mom good things, loving things, things that will make her feel better about herself and our situation and me. I feel like she deserves that.

And I want to be cruel, to say fuck off and leave me the

hell alone, stop acting like I'm the world's worst son and concentrate on your own self. *I don't deserve that.*

She leaves and I've said nothing.

I look out the side door and see Priya on the ground with Ginger beside her. My heart beats a little faster. I think it's time I give this alien a vacation.

2:02 P.M.

Kennywood is our area's summer go-to place. It's got roller coasters and bumper cars, funnel cakes and deep-fried Oreos—and I plan to introduce Priya to all of it.

The sights and sounds can be overwhelming. I remember when I was a little kid, Mom and Dad brought me there for the first time. Everything seemed so big, so fast, so loud.

Mom took me on the baby water rides and the trolley, but Dad insisted on the adult rides. I was tall for my age so I made the cutoff for most of them. I think Mom was worried riding the big coasters would scar me for life, but it did just the opposite: It created an appetite in me for bigger-taller-faster. Give me more loops, more dips, more sharp turns and quick plunges.

It was a safe way to be scared.

But when I look into Priya's eyes, I see she's actually terrified. "You okay?"

She answers by gripping my fingers tighter. "I don't know what this place is."

"Well, it's an amusement park. I told you. We just, you know, have fun." I'm aware of others eavesdropping and I turn my back to them and try to keep my voice down.

"What is that?" Priya whispers back as she ogles the Racer.

"A roller coaster." How do you explain a thing like a roller coaster? "It goes pretty high and pretty fast and it's meant to be scary, I guess, but you won't get hurt." I point to the coaster. "Watch."

Her head tilts back as she watches two trains of cars slowly chug up the first incline. People wave and woo-hoo and slap the hands of the passengers in the train next to them. Just as the first car tips over the edge, I turn to look at Priya. Her eyes grow wide and white as she follows the plunging coasters. The passengers scream and pull their arms back in as the coaster whips around corners and dives and drops. Priya buries her head in my neck and clutches my waist.

Ah, now I get that whole horror-movie date thing.

"Don't worry, it'll be fine. I'll be right next to you."

"What if we fall?"

I laugh and point again to the coaster. "We'll fall but then we'll go back up again. And then fall and go back up. It'll be just like you're in your rocket ship."

She scowls. "That is *not* how space travel works at all."

We're getting closer to the front of the line. "Come on," I urge Priya. "I won't let anything happen to you."

After another hot minute of waiting, it's our turn. We're in the very first car. When we were eleven and twelve, in the summers when Mrs. Aoki ferried the three of us to the mall and the lake and here, Brian and Em and I loved this coaster. We would time the line just right so we could sit in the front seats of the first cars in each of the trains, climbing the first hill side by side and "racing" to the top. Like idiots, we would throw our hands in the air and feel the initial drop all the way to our feet.

Priya slides in with a nervous smile.

"When the bar locks, hold on with both hands, okay?" I tell her. She nods, still anxious, so I wrap one arm around her shoulder and pull her closer to me.

The Racer was my first coaster too. I wonder if this is what I was like with my dad. Scared? Probably. Excited? Definitely. But I trusted him with my life. I knew he wouldn't let anything happen to me.

And I won't let anything happen to Priya, either.

"Here we go!"

The slow rise, inch by inch, is the best part, if you ask

me. Especially on a wooden coaster. The *tick-tick-tick* of the chains as the car is pulled up to the top makes my heart beat faster. Beside me, I think Priya has stopped breathing. She's got her lips pressed together and her eyes squeezed shut, her chin pulled back into her neck like a turtle. I lean over and kiss her on the cheek and she looks up at me and smiles, relaxing immediately. Is that all it takes to ease a troubled mind? A single, simple kiss? I do it again. And again. Until Priya giggles and blushes.

Just as the car reaches the top, I feel her lean into me and I hold her tighter. It means I don't have free hands to hold over my head but that's okay. This is better.

We plunge over the drop, escaping the rest of the world. For a split second, we are lighter than air, floating and falling, and for the next minute and a half, we will defy gravity. It will pull us to Earth but we'll twist away, over and over and over again.

3:34 P.M.

We are like noodles after the third coaster, our arms and legs limp and our skin clammy. Priya rests her head on my shoulder, and the warmth of our bodies so close to each other makes my head swim.

"Matthew?" Priya asks. She doesn't look so great. She squints and winces against obvious pain, holding both hands to her temples. Must have been that last coaster.

"You okay?"

"Matthew, my head really hurts. Do you have any medicine?"

I dig my hands into my pockets and come up empty. I should have thought ahead, should have brought snacks and medicine or even just some water, but I was anxious to get out of the house after this morning's fiasco with Mom.

A crowd swirls around us, hurrying to get to the next ride, the next food cart, the next souvenir shop. Priya looks like she's about to pass out.

All these people? Someone has to have some meds.

A group of kids run past. Way too young.

A trio of frat boys. They probably have *something* but it won't be legal.

More kids, younger and younger. Where are parents when you need them?

Finally I spot a woman pushing a stroller. She looks weary and worn and I'm betting she gets headaches a lot.

"Excuse me? Do you have any Advil or Tylenol?" I ask her. "It's for my girlfr—my friend. She has a, uh, a migraine."

The woman glances at Priya and the skepticism on her face gives way to sympathy. She digs her hand in a purse that's wrapped around her stroller, fishing out a round brown pill and an oblong white one. "Here. They're ibuprofen of some kind. These places are the worst," she adds.

Priya accepts them like they're jewels. "Thank you."

The woman leaves and Priya glances up at me. "How did you know who to ask?"

"I don't know . . . I guess I just tried to imagine what someone who had Advil would look like."

Think like a cat.

After we find some water for Priya to wash down the

pills, I look for a bench to sit on, but every spot in the shade is taken. I steer us through the crowds, navigating around strollers and big backpacks and kids trying to balance ice cream cones, and find the only place to sit out of the sun.

The merry-go-round.

I jump aboard and lift Priya by the waist, flinging her into a seat as the last of the riders hop on. When we were kids, we'd ride the painted ponies, naturally. No one but old people sat in the chairs, or "chariots" as they're called.

With Priya cuddled next to me, I guess I don't mind being an old person. She sighs and closes her eyes as the carousel whirls and the Wurlitzer plays. I can't remember the last time I was on this thing; Em would never ride it. Too slow, too boring. Brian long ago lost interest in most of the rides here, preferring the gasoline smell and adrenaline rush of dirt bikes.

After a couple of turns, we relax against the padded seat and I pull Priya alongside me so she can rest her chin on my chest. The breeze of the carousel brings the scent of sugary cotton candy and chili fries.

I feel Priya's palm on my thigh, surprisingly cool through my jeans, and she lifts her face to mine. Her lips part slightly, giving me a glimpse of teeth and tongue just as she reaches behind my neck to pull me closer. I feel her mouth on mine and I kiss her back.

This is a thousand times better than those stupid horses. No wonder the old people sit in these chairs.

Priya's fingers stroke my chin and neck and she pulls back just far enough to look me in the eyes. "I like this place," she says. And then she kisses me again.

This place—does she mean Kennywood? The carousel? Or Earth?

The organ music, drowning out the rest of the park, the rest of the world, has never sounded so lovely. The air drips with its mechanical notes as we whirl around and around and around. A thousand lights dazzle, dozens of painted horses gallop—all to entertain Priya and me in our fancy chariot.

When the ride stops, we stay on for a second trip.

5:59 P.M.

I try not to think about Priya while I'm in the shower, but it's hard to wash my legs and forget how she stroked her hand along my thigh when we were on the carousel. It's hard to shampoo my hair and forget how she ran her fingers through it as she pressed her lips to my neck. And it's impossible to lather up my chest and forget how she melted in my arms when I kissed her on the roller coaster.

It's not that I have a one-track mind. That would mean there's some sort of path or logic to it. Nope. It's just one big pile of sex in my head.

Priya is in my room when I get out of the bathroom with a fresh shave and a healthy slather of deodorant. She's sitting at my desk—there *is* a desk underneath the crap—studying something, a book or a magazine, I guess.

"I was thinking we could go to a movie tomorrow," I say. "There's a mall just outside of town that's kind of run-down, but they have a theater with three screens."

She doesn't move or act at all interested.

Over her shoulder I see what she's poring over: Dad's collection of newspaper clippings from 1965. I quickly close the folder and snatch it out from under her nose.

"Matthew, excuse me, but I was—"

"I don't know how you found these, but they're really old and not, you know, useful." Honestly, I can't even recall *where* in my room this folder was: my desk? my closet? under my bed? I tuck it under my arm.

Priya follows me as I go to the closet to grab a fresh T-shirt from the shelf. "Those articles are from the crash. Why can't I see them? They are public record, yes?"

"Well, yes, but—"

"Then I could go to a library and ask someone for them."

"A library?"

"Or I could directly contact the newspapers in which they were originally published."

"If they still exist."

"Why don't you want me to see them?"

I sigh and stare at the T-shirts on my shelf. Blue, gray, yellow? Nike logo? Adidas logo? Phillies logo? What am I trying to say to the world with my clothing? "Fine," I tell her, and hand her the folder over my shoulder.

"Thank you."

I grab a plain gray shirt that has no pit stains and pull it over my head. "The whole town . . . it's like everyone went crazy for one night."

Priya, sitting on my bed, tilts her head to one side. "Your town was a collective witness. They saw the ship crash."

I hold up a finger. "No. They saw the aftermath of the crash. Or whatever it was. They never saw anything flying through the air, never saw anything actually hit the ground. The earth shook, people ran. There was a fire. The end."

Priya places a finger under her chin in thought, staring at the clippings.

"It was the middle of the night. I mean, how could they know what they were looking at? Half of them had just woken up and none of them agreed on exactly what happened. Some said it was a fireball falling from the sky. Some said it didn't catch fire until it hit the ground. It was round, then triangular, then shaped like a cone. It had wheels or wings, was black or silver or copper, depending on who you asked." I stop, winded by my speech. My hands are trembling and I feel a hitch in my breath. "Waste of time. A stupid waste."

I want to believe.

"You do believe," Priya says to me.

"No." I shake my head. "No, I *did* believe. I believed in my dad."

"You still believe."

Priya smiles at me, such a knowing, intelligent gaze. She sure doesn't *look* crazy.

"He was a fraud," I tell her. "He got caught up in his minor celebrity. In people liking him, people who didn't even know him. He cared more about their opinions than mine."

She takes my face in her hands and I feel her touch all the way down to my knees. I just want to wrap myself around her. I want her lips at my neck and my ears and my chin. I want her hands everywhere.

I want to forget the past and imagine my future.

"Priya," I whisper in her ear, "are you really who you say you are?"

"I am exactly what you're thinking I am."

7:35 P.M.

I sit across from Priya in the living room, watching her eat pizza in my Phillies T-shirt and a pair of Mom's shorts. I gave her something to wear while I wash her tutu and top after our long afternoon at the amusement park. The clothes swim on her but it doesn't matter: she could have a parka and jeans on and I wouldn't care. She dazzles me like the lights on the Kennywood grand carousel no matter what she's wearing.

After she polishes off the last slice—splitting it with Ginger, her new best friend—she settles back on the couch just half a cushion away.

"I will definitely miss this food of yours," she says, patting her belly.

"Maybe you can teach them how to make pizza," I say, tapping my temple like she often does. "Your data collection must have something in there."

She laughs and leans into me, her hair falling across my chin. I want to grab her shoulders and pull her to me, to not let her sit back on her side of the couch, but somehow I manage to keep my hands still.

She regards me, her lips upturned in a smile. "Matthew, I have only the taste to share with them. The sensation of eating the pizza."

"And what is the sensation of eating a pizza?"

"It's . . . not unlike sliding through a wormhole."

That cracks me up and my laugh fills the room. "What does *that* mean?"

Priya's grin is steady. "When your ship passes through a wormhole, you feel the change in time and space in your whole body."

"And that's like eating a pizza?"

"The pizza is the wormhole. When I eat it, my whole body shifts. I taste the saltiness of the cheese combined with the tang of the tomatoes at the very moment my teeth crunch into the crust. This is sensed instantaneously. There is no separation of flavors. They are there all at once, an explosion not unlike the sudden shift in the time-space continuum in a wormhole." She smiles serenely and spreads open her palms. "Do you see?"

I shake my head. "No. And now I wish we had more pizza."

Priya takes my hand in both of hers, startling me. On the cushion between us, her fingers play with mine, tangle and untangle as if they were thick strands of hair, or the willow branches down by the creek. "Matthew, I will have to leave. Probably tonight."

"Tonight?" Sudden panic grips my throat. My brain just does not want to assimilate this bit of information, no matter how many times she tells me.

We both look out the window, our eyes finding the setting sun. How did it get so late?

"It *is* late," she says, reading my mind again. She bends down to my hand and brushes her cheek and lips against it. "Mmmm . . . you smell like pizza."

"My favorite cologne," I say. As she starts to rise from the couch, I pull her back. "We can order another one. Another pie for your trip back."

She shakes her head. "That was enough. We will be in suspended animation for the return home," she says matter-of-factly. "We will not be able to eat pizza." She gently disengages her hand from mine. "Would you get my clothes for me? I can't travel in this outfit."

"Not your usual uniform?" I tease her.

She scowls at me. "We don't have uniforms."

I head for the basement, calling back to her. "No? Space

travel isn't like *Star Trek*? No one-piece-unitard things?"

Priya laughs. "That show is very unrealistic. Space is *not* like that."

"Well, it *is* the future," I say.

Of all the space worlds, I like the Trekverse best. Peace and community and a holodeck for all your fantasies. I'd ride into the final frontier if I had a replicator and a transporter.

When I come back from the laundry room with Priya's fresh-smelling clothes, I find her collapsed on the floor of the living room. Her legs are twisted under her and her head lolls to one side. Ginger paces back and forth, whining.

"Priya!" I drop everything and run. I pick her up and carry her to the couch. Her long arms and legs are like the tentacles of an octopus, all rubbery and out of control.

Her eyes open, lashes blinking against the light and me. Confusion furrows her brow and her lips part as if she were about to say something.

"Priya? Are you okay? Can you hear me?"

Finally, she nods, forehead relaxing as she recognizes me. "I'm . . ." Her voice trails to a mumble.

"What did you say?"

"I . . . I will . . ." And then, more confidently: "I will be fine." She pushes herself to a sitting position and slowly swings her legs over the side of the couch, trying to get up.

"Whoa, hang on."

She shrugs off my help, irritated. "I'm fine, Matthew!

Leave me alone!" She launches her body off the couch, as if defying me to stop her.

I don't and she stumbles forward, catching her hand on the arm of the sofa and sort of lurching back and forth, drunkenly, before settling in an upright position. She winces and her hand goes to her head, massaging her temple in a circle.

Are you okay? I want to ask, but bite my tongue. She doesn't want my help. It's weird, this sudden change in her. She even walks differently. Her gait is awkward—more awkward than usual—and her head twitches as she cringes inwardly, at something going on internally.

I follow her at a distance out to the kitchen, picking up her clothes along the way. She pauses at the door, looking out at the field. Her hands grip the doorframe and her back shudders. She breathes heavily, her shoulders rising and falling. I don't think she's crying. Is she crying?

"Priya—"

"Matthew . . . I have a headache again. May I have an aspirin?"

"Just one?"

She clears her throat but doesn't turn to me. "Maybe more."

I leave her clothes on the kitchen table. "Yeah, sure." I hurry to the first-floor bathroom and grab at the bottles of painkillers. "You know, maybe you need to see a doctor if you keep having headaches," I call to her. "I know you don't want to talk to my mom, but she knows stuff about stuff. I mean, it's probably just the heat or something, but all those meds aren't that good for you." I run the water in the sink until it's cold and fill a glass. "I read once that you can do some serious damage to your liver if you take too much—"

From the hallway, I see she's gone. Back door wide open. Tutu and dog missing.

I really need to stop turning my back on this girl. Something always seems to happen when I'm not looking.

The sun is at the edge of the horizon when I get up to the field. Priya stands directly in the center of it, a stick figure against the glorious orange glow that fills the sky. Her head is angled to one side, and she cradles her cheek in her palm, her elbow crooked into her waist.

I hold the water out to her and pour some pills into my hand. She cups my hand in hers and tilts it toward her mouth; her lips brush my skin as her tongue flicks the pills from my palm. I feel a shiver roll up my spine and the hairs on the back of my neck stand straight up.

She finishes the water with an *ahh*. "I feel better."

"That was fast."

"I felt better as soon as I came out here."

"Must be the fresh air."

"Oh, Matthew . . . ," she says with a shake of her head. *You're so naive*, I hear in her voice, and that kind of pisses me off.

"What?"

"It's the field. You know that."

"It's not. And I don't." I sound like a belligerent child. "The fucking field is just a field," I add, profanity being proof I'm not a kid. *So there.*

"You're not as skeptical as you think you are," she tells me confidently.

"Like you know me?"

"I do. You love that telescope," she says. "You loved it when you were a child. You looked at the stars, side by side with your dad, and imagined what was out there, what was beyond the Earth and the moon."

I shrug. I have a telescope. Seems logical I'd like looking at things through it.

"And you wished you could go out there. You and your dad."

"You know, you can stop talking about him."

She stares at me blankly.

"Yeah, the stars were cool. They *are* cool. And I like looking. And I like imagining." I look up at the moon that is beginning to appear in the sky. It's that hazy time between sunset and night, that twilight moment when the world around us starts to shift. Which are we, I wonder, day or night?

"What did you imagine when you looked up at those stars?" she asks me.

"Me?"

"Yes, when you and your father watched the skies. What

did you imagine was out there?" Her voice reaches to me, drawing me out like little Boo from under the Aokis' porch.

I glance over at the telescope as if I could see my dad and me, years ago, when Ginger was just a pup frolicking in the dry grass.

Billions and billions of stars.

"I guess . . . I guess I imagined what it would be like to be out there, to sail from one planet to another. Not like *Star Trek*," I add. "But real astronauts, real explorers."

"And what did you think it would be like?"

"Magical," I say. "Exciting. Transformative."

Priya murmurs, "It is all those things."

Before my dad ever had a blog, I was his biggest fan. I was his first follower. I believed the field we were in was a wonderful, magical place. I believed the fact that the aliens had landed there meant anything was possible, even for someone as small as me.

He told me to look to the skies. We were like the stars that glittered and glowed. We could find ourselves among them if we just looked hard enough. We could do great things. We could make a difference. We could be special.

But I grew up and things changed.

"I'm not stupid," I tell Priya. "I know what's real and what's . . . not."

"Real, unreal, Matthew—"

"The stars are real, the planets are real." I point up at the sky. "We are real."

"I know these things about you," Priya says. "Because we are connected. Like my people at home."

"Priya, I don't think that's it," I say with a laugh and a shrug.

And then she kisses me. A full-on, mouth-to-mouth, resuscitate-the-dead kiss. Her tongue explores mine in a tangle of tastes—pizza and soda and the bitter aspirin dust. My arms wrap around her back and hers around my waist and we fold into each other like a pair of origami cranes. The last thing I see when I close my eyes is the fading sun over the field.

When I open them again, we are on the ground, my shirts—both the one I was wearing and the one Priya had on—are under us, the thinnest barrier between our skin and the dry earth. I run my hands along Priya's side, from her thigh to the slope of her hip and waist, trailing my fingers up her arm and across her collarbone. My hand leads my lips and I kiss that same curving path from thigh to neck.

Priya's fingers and then her mouth caress a trail up my leg and waist but her lips don't stop at my neck; I feel her tongue gently lick my earlobe and her teeth nibble behind my ear.

I do the same and she giggles.

"Ticklish?"

"Keep going."

Don't have to tell me twice.

I roll onto my back and pull Priya on top of me. Her hair falls across my bare chest and that should tickle, but no, it doesn't. It feels weird and amazing and a little awkward, but mostly amazing and kind of scary and definitely absolutely fucking amazing.

I hold her by the hips as she rocks against me and I press her chest to mine. Our hearts thunder together, blocking out voices, cars, dogs, logic, anything that is not here, is not now, is not between us at this moment. I don't care about anything else.

I gaze into her eyes, afraid to look, afraid to see what's in there.

Fragments of thoughts echo in my head.

She barely knows me, she can't love me.

She's crazy, she's beautiful.

She's leaving.

She's leaving.

She's leaving.

My hand pulls her head to mine, and I inhale her, and my tongue goes deep inside her mouth. As we kiss, I see the birth of a new star far off in the universe, an explosion of color in the empty black expanse of space.

We created it.

We are the center of the universe.

3:06 A.M.

The stars are our blanket.

I stretch my arms above me as if I could expand myself beyond the Milky Way, fingers reaching toward Mars, Neptune, Venus—and Priya's home.

Okay, sex with Priya has made me corny and sentimental and a little bit stupid.

That didn't happen with Em. We just laughed a lot after the first time because it sure didn't take long. And then we fooled around and did it again and that second time was better, but it didn't turn me into a poetry lover. Didn't turn me into a *lover* at all. The next day I didn't feel any different. I wasn't changed.

But this was . . .

Magical. Exciting. Transformative.

Star stuff.

I roll onto my side, feel Priya tucked into me, her back against my chest, and I let my arm dangle over her waist. I can feel her heart beating through her spine and a thin layer of sweat on her skin. I'm sure my whole body is drenched in perspiration. That's gross—

"You're not gross," she says, answering my thought.

"No? You don't think so?"

"It's a natural function."

"For you too, I see." I trail my finger down her shoulder, through slick, wet drops. I flick my tongue out to taste them. "Mmmm, salty."

Priya laughs as if I'd tickled her. "Are you happy?"

"Am I . . . ? Well, uh, yeah, aren't you?"

"Oh yes, I am. Also a little cold," she adds.

Our clothes are scattered behind us, and I gather them up without actually standing. We dress side by side, lying on the ground, and stay there, looking up at the sky. I take Priya's hand and point it at the cluster of bright lights around the moon high above us.

"Most people think those are stars," I say.

"They're planets. You call them Venus and Mars," she says, dragging my hand from one shining beacon to the next.

"*I* do? What do *you* call them?"

"I told you, we have no language. We simply communicate to one another. Our thoughts are shared."

As I twine my fingers around Priya's, I think how beautiful it sounds when she talks about it. Shared thoughts. Communicating without speaking. How different would life be if we didn't have to worry about saying the wrong thing? Doing the wrong thing? Thinking someone meant one thing when they meant something else entirely?

Like *I promise*.

"That's how the Universe works," Priya says. "We are all connected. We help one another through the power of our thoughts."

The cynic in me snorts. I can't help it. "Sounds like prayer."

Priya thinks a moment. "I suppose you might call it that."

Yeah, okay, I have to laugh. "What, you pray to each other? Like, to God?"

I feel Priya smile. "We are all God."

I push myself to sitting and stare into Priya's face to see if she's messing with me. "We are all God. You? Me? How about Ginger?"

My dog lifts her head, thinking I'm calling her for treats.

"Matthew, this is well-known throughout the Universe," she says, a bit perturbed by my ignorance. "Just because something can't be seen doesn't mean it can't be believed." She aims a critical eye at me. "You seem to have a hard time with concepts that must be taken upon faith."

"You mean, like God, aliens—"

"Love." She smiles. "You can't see it but you believe it exists."

I feel my cheeks color. "Love is a theory."

"Like gravity?"

"I can't prove that either of those things exist."

"Yet you believe the periodic table of elements exists, yes? You believe hydrogen and nitrogen and plutonium exist?"

I feel my head nod. The basics of chemistry. That was one class I didn't fail.

"Then you know that every element in the Universe, every atom, every particle has always existed. Which means *we* have always existed. We are God."

I spread open my arms wide. "I am immortal! Bow down to me!"

Priya laughs. "Stars are born, burn out, go supernova—and are reborn. Everything in the Universe dies and is reborn over and over again." She sits up, grabs hold of my arms, and pulls them around her and we tumble back onto the ground. When I open my eyes, I am looking up into hers. They are vulnerable yet wise, calm, confident.

I've seen that look before: on my dad. Before he got caught up in the voices of the crazies, he was excited about science, about the possibilities of the Universe.

"And our souls?" I ask her. "Do we have them? What happens to our souls when we die? Are they reborn too?"

She looks at me with a question on her face. "Soul." She rolls the word around in her mouth. "Your spirit is energy and energy never dies. It's—"

"It's merely converted," I say. Because I know that is true. That is physics. Energy can't ever be created or destroyed.

"We are energy," she says. "We are matter. We are not created or destroyed." And then she pulls me closer and presses her lips against mine and I feel a surge of energy between us.

This won't ever die, I think wildly. We, us, this moment will never go away. It might be converted into something else—love? memory?—but it exists forever.

I gently release her and her eyes flutter a few times, sleepily. "Are you tired?"

"I must stay awake," she says, trying to sit back up. "My ship—"

"I'll watch for it."

"You?"

"What, you think I don't know what a spaceship looks like?" I kiss her forehead and her eyes close again. "I've got my eyes on the skies." In a minute, she's asleep and I slide my arm out from under her neck.

A few yards away near the telescope is Priya's bag. I crawl quietly across the field to retrieve it and place it within arm's length of her, in case she wakes up and feels for it. Naturally I grab it from the wrong end and something tumbles out.

Priya's notebook.

It feels dense in the palm of my hand, heavy with import. To look inside this, to peel back the layers of *this*, would be an invasion of privacy, wouldn't it? It would be like opening up her mind and poking around inside.

Or would it?

The notebook is nothing special: smooth black leather cover with lined pages. It's worn and soft, like a well-loved jacket, and it has an elastic band attached to the spine to hold it closed. You'd think something as important as this is to Priya would be kept under lock and key instead of a thin strip of coated rubber.

On the first page is her name. Or rather, a sentence that declares her name: "My name is Priya."

Directly below that is a series of symbols I've never seen before.

That's it. That's the first page. Okay.

Page two. Whoa. Line after line is filled with words spaced very tightly together, hardly any blank areas between or around the letters.

Red means stop.

A dime is worth more than a penny.

Hot dogs are NOT dogs.

The third page is the same, although the pen color is different.

Do not pick flowers from a strange garden.

Do not eat flowers from a strange garden.

Okay. . . .

And on and on. Some of the most inane things are written in varying degrees of penmanship. Some lines are printed very clearly while others are sloppily scripted. Black and blue pen, a few lines in pencil, but very little white space.

Drawings, too. Sketches of faces and eyes and hands, cars and cats and houses. A lamp, a teapot, a railroad crossing sign. Symbols below and their English translations, from what I can tell.

I flip to the very last page where she has written, "Ginger is a dog." But "dog" is crossed out and "Labrador retriever" is written above it. In the margin, there is a hastily drawn image of a dog, *my* dog, with her wide face and her runty body.

But why?

Obviously this was new information to her and she needed to write it down in order to remember it. And the only reason these sorts of basic things would be new to her is if she wasn't from a place that had them.

A place without dogs. A place without railroad crossing signs. A place without teapots or houses or cars. A place where the color red did *not* mean stop.

Where on earth would a place like that exist?

Just because you can't see it doesn't mean you can't believe in it.

The realization of what this could mean stuns me like a punch to the jaw. Are these crib notes? Cheat sheets? Important information a visitor to our planet would need to know?

No. Like, no fucking way. That is seriously not possible.

I hold up the notebook, inspecting it from all angles as if I might read into it some other explanation.

A normal girl doesn't carry a notebook like this.

A normal *human* girl doesn't carry a notebook like this.

I want to slap myself silly. In fact, a stupid little giggle bubbles up in my throat and I have to swallow it like spit. No. Just no. And no.

She is not an alien. She is not from another planet.

But the notes . . . who keeps notes like that?

I glance over at Priya, who is on her back, hands by her sides, softly snoring. "Are you crazy?" I whisper. "Or are you what you say you are?"

I want to believe.

About a year ago, long before we had any inkling Dad was going to cheat on Mom, let alone hit the road with Carol, my uncle and his wife were over for dinner. It was a weird, middle-of-the-week get-together, something they didn't usually do. While Brian and I were sitting in my room, all four of the adults downstairs were drinking with every course. Whiskey with their Doritos and dip, white wine with their salads, beer with their baked chicken. By the time they got to dessert, they were thoroughly wasted, which we discovered when we came downstairs scrounging for a snack.

We found Mom sitting on Dad's lap while Carol and Jack were leaning into each other and making goofy faces.

Brian and I couldn't stop laughing at the four of them as we inhaled all their apple pie à la mode and leftover chips.

Jack saw us and immediately straightened up, pretending he was actually sober. "Hey there, kiddo, what's going on? How's school?"

Normally I would have rolled my eyes at the *kiddo* bullshit, but I just shrugged and shoved more chips in my mouth. "'SallrightIguess."

"You don't do much of that stargazing with your dad anymore, do you?" he asked with a nod at my father.

"Uh, no, not really." More chips. More pie.

"Then you won't miss it when he sells the telescopes."

"Sell . . . you're selling the telescopes?"

My dad, his cheeks red from the booze, grinned, but it was halfhearted. "Yep. I'm selling it all." He threw his hand in the air like he was tossing confetti.

"Why?"

Mom interrupted. "He doesn't need it anymore. He's getting a job!"

My heart pumped. "You are? Well, that's . . . that's

awesome." I was confused. My dad loved his telescope and his stargazing. Why would he get rid of it all? "What kind of job are you getting?"

"He's gonna sell cars with me," Jack said proudly.

"Cars?" Brian blurted out, his mouth filled with ice cream. "DJ, you can't sell cars."

My father looked sheepish, like he knew Brian was right. He couldn't sell cars. I couldn't even imagine him in a tie, or a shirt that had buttons.

"He can do anything he sets his mind to," Mom declared. "First the telescopes are going and then the rest of the junk out there." She met my dad's gaze and smiled. "That workshop's going back to what it used to be."

"A wine cellar," Jack said. He high-fived Mom.

A wine cellar. A job for Dad. No more stars. What was going on here? Had I fallen through to another dimension?

As my teeth ground through another handful of Doritos and orange cheese dust coated my fingers, I watched my parents plant sloppy kisses on each other. I was glad my father was finally getting a job but disappointed the telescopes were going away—and with them, the heart of my dad's existence. I knew he'd brought it on himself. He'd done nothing memorable, nothing substantial, in the past ten or fifteen or maybe even twenty years. He needed to move on, move forward, leave this crap behind.

But part of that crap involved *me*.

DAY SIX

7:23 A.M.

By the time I stumble into the kitchen, it's past dawn, but Mom is already gone. I look around for a note telling me she had an early shift at the hospital or an emergency.

Hmm . . . nothing on the counter or the fridge door, but she left the coffeepot on so there's a crusty layer of burned black sludge on the bottom.

Face facts, Matty. That's your note.

"Thanks, Mom. Love you too."

No sooner have I cleaned up and made fresh coffee than the phone rings in the living room. The landline? Who the hell is calling on the landline? I almost don't know what I'm hearing. It's been forever since anyone has actually called it. I snatch it off the cradle like it's a bomb.

"Yeah."

"Matty, hey."

"Em?" I freeze and stare at the phone. "You're calling me?"

"Duh."

"I mean, on the home phone. This isn't my cell."

Emily sighs, the weight of a thousand worlds on her shoulders. "Nothing gets past you, huh, dipshit?"

"So thanks for calling and insulting me."

"You wanna go to the lake with me and Toad?"

"Excuse me?"

"The lake? You wanna go?"

My eyes squint and find the clock on the other side of the room. It's not even eight. "What are you doing back? I thought you were at your gran's."

She sighs. "Long story."

"So you're back."

"Are you not listening? Yes, we're back. And we're going to the lake and we're inviting you."

"Um, I have a friend visiting."

"That girl? Bring her."

I take the phone with me to the kitchen and look out the back door. Priya and Ginger are asleep in the field. A blush comes to my cheeks when I think of her—of us.

"Going once, going twice . . ."

"No thanks."

"No?"

I feel my shoulders shrug. "Nah. We're good." *We*.

Yeah, that's what I said. Priya and me. *We're* good.

"But—"

"Gotta go." I click off the phone and dump it on the table.

Did I just turn down Emily?

Yup.

Did it feel good?

No.

It felt *awesome*.

I go back to the coffee and hum the theme song to *The Twilight Zone* a couple of times, and the phone rings again. We really should get caller ID.

"Hello?"

"We'll drive," Em says, as if the conversation never ended.

"Yeah, no. Not interested."

"Why not?"

"Emily. No." I pace the kitchen with the phone, still not quite comprehending why Emily is being so obtuse.

Maybe *she* doesn't like hearing no either.

Em makes a little snorting sound. "Look, I'm trying to be nice."

Is she? Does she feel bad she treated me like crap?

Outside in the field, I see my dog slowly circle Priya, pausing to stretch her back and legs every couple of feet.

"Em, I gotta jump, all right? Have fun at the lake."

This time I hang up before she can get a last word in . . .

. . . and then she calls back. I swipe it off the counter before it rings a second time.

"No, Emily. Not interested."

Silence and then . . . "Junior, hey."

"Dad?" I feel a huge rock drop right into my stomach.

"Yeah, hi." His voice brightens. "You doing okay?"

"Am I . . . ?" I hold the phone out and stare at it as if I could telegraph to my father my sincere inability to believe he's calling me. "Yeah, I guess."

"That's good. You're taking care of your mom?"

Oh my god, seriously? Like he's on a trip out of town and I'm watching an invalid?

I ask him the same thing I asked Em. "You know you're calling the landline?"

"Oh right, yeah, I, uh, your number is in my old cell."
Which is here.

He cough-laughs a bit sheepishly. "I could only remember the house number."

"So . . . I'm kind of on my way out the door." Literally. I am literally leaving this very second.

On the other end of the line, I hear his clothing rustle as if he were juggling the phone in his shirt. Where is he calling from? Without caller ID I can't even get an area code.

Not that I care.

"Oh sure, okay, well, could you tell your mom I took the lockbox with me?"

"Uh-huh."

"Do you know if she and Jack were looking for it?"

"Uh-huh."

"Okay, well, they probably want the deed to the farm."

"Yeah, I guess." I place my hand on the door, pressing my palm against the glass. Outside, Ginger and Priya are both standing in the field, probably wondering where I am.

"So you're on your way out, huh?"

"Yup."

"Hanging with Toad?"

"We're going out to the lake, actually. I'm leaving right now, actually."

"Actually?"

"Yeah, actually." I feel my internal temperature rise ten degrees. The hand holding the phone starts to get slick with sweat.

"Okay, well, let me give you my new number in case your mom . . . or you know, *you* want to call me in the future."

"Uh-huh."

He slowly recites the number while I pour myself a cup of coffee and pretend I'm interested. I hum the *Twilight Zone* theme song again in my head. That tune never gets old.

"Uh-huh, okay, yup, got it," I tell my dad.

He sounds relieved when I assure him I've got all ten digits in the right sequence. "Thanks, Junior. I appreciate it."

I wait for him to tell me why he left, to apologize for leaving, to say it was a mistake, but he just keeps thanking me.

I let the air between us grow heavy and stale, wait for him to puncture it, which he does because he can't stand the quiet.

"I'll let you go."

"Yup."

"Call me, okay?"

"Yup."

He hangs up—finally—and I shove the conversation out of my mind.

I pull my phone out of my pocket and text Emily: *meet u at lake*

12:07 P.M.

Priya and I get to the lake before the kids and moms have left, which means towel space is at a premium. The only spot we find is far from the lifeguard tower, which, since the beautiful and out-of-reach Miranda is working, will not be a satisfactory location for Brian. Oh well.

I spread a couple of towels side by side and encourage Priya to sit down, but she's gawking openly at the people on the beach, at the children playing in the sand and splashing in the water. She said she's never been to a lake before. How can you live in Pennsylvania and not see a lake? We have, like, a million of them.

I take off my sneakers and socks and tuck them into the

canvas tote bag I brought our stuff in. It's already close to ninety and humid as shit.

I love watching Priya. Her eyes are wide with discovery; she drinks in everything and everyone she sees, from the little kids and their sand castles to the moms and dads with lobster-red skin because they used all their sunscreen on their children.

She's like a golden willow bending softly with the breeze; her nose wrinkles with the scents of summer. Her tutu tangles up in her legs and she dances near the gentle surf, kicking up her heels and running away when the water threatens to lap at her toes. The little kids laugh and clap their hands as they run with her.

I could watch her forever.

Five minutes later, Brian and Emily arrive—and I feel strangely disappointed. I kind of hoped they wouldn't show up at all.

"Dude, lookin' 1985," I say to my friend, who's wearing a pair of mirrored aviator glasses and a black T-shirt over his board shorts. When I look at him, I see my pasty self staring back.

His eyebrows lift over the top of his glasses and he grins. "She's here."

I glance over my shoulder to Priya, who is playing at the water's edge. How could he know?

Emily comes up behind him, dragging their bag of towels and other lakeside crap. "He found the lifeguard schedule online," she tells me with a note of wonder in her voice. She sounds almost proud of her brother, as if he were a toddler who'd managed to use the toilet instead of crapping his pants as usual.

"Oh, you mean Miranda," I say.

"Now I'll know every day she's here," Brian says as he stares open-mouthed at the lifeguard tower. Miranda is wearing an orange bathing suit, and her black hair is twisted in a braid down her back. Her eagle eyes scan the horizon for an errant swimmer. Her partner is Eric Miller, so Em should be happy. He's in orange too. Both have superb tans and toned bodies. Whatever. Muscles are so overrated.

Beside me, Emily spreads a towel and kicks off her flip-flops. Her eyes count the towels already on the sand, and she looks at me. "You brought your friend?"

"The girl who's crazy beautiful," Brian says without taking his gaze from Miranda. "Or did you say crazy *and* beautiful? I think I was stoned when you texted me that night."

I avoid looking at Em but it doesn't matter, I can feel her eyes on me, drilling into me. "Is this her? The one with white hair?" she asks.

I nod, and Em nods too. Then very subtly, she turns and looks around her, immediately finds Priya by the water.

"She must be hot," Emily says.

"Why? You think the only reason I'd bring a girl to the

lake is 'cause she's hot? You think I'm that superficial? She happens to be pretty smart, too."

"Whoa." Emily looks up at me, her face a blank. "Are you done, Mr. Paranoid?"

"Me?"

"I meant she must be *hot*, like physically too warm. She's wearing a heavy skirt and a T-shirt. Why doesn't she have a bathing suit?"

"Oh. She, um, she didn't bring one. This was kind of a spur-of-the-moment thing." I watch Priya hop back from the water when a gentle wave laps at her. Her musical laugh carries and I laugh too, infected by it. "Do you really think that skirt is heavy?"

Em looks at me like I'm crazy. "Duh. It's a *skirt*. Look at all those layers."

Huh. I thought they were like cotton candy—light and fluffy and feathery. It never occurred to me it would be warm. I call to Priya and she turns with a brilliant smile. Even Emily smiles in return. How could you not? She looks so happy. She has a hard time walking in the sand—who wouldn't? I jump up and help her back to the towels.

Naturally, Brian comes over to meet her. I slap at him and point at his glasses. "Dude. Take those things off."

"Hey, I'm Brian."

"I'm Emily."

"I know," Priya says. "He thinks about you all the time."

"Excuse me?"

"She means 'talk'—I talk about you all the time. This is Priya."

"Let her sit, Matty," Em says. She makes space for Priya on the towel between us. As usual, Priya sits with her legs straight in front of her, hands in her lap. "So where are you from?"

"She's just visiting," I say quickly.

"From where?" Em asks again.

Priya opens her mouth to answer, but I jump in again. "Not far."

She looks at me sharply. "That isn't true. I come from very far away."

"Philadelphia!" Brian shouts. When his sister sighs, he puts his hands on his hips. "What? Philly's far away."

"You moron. She means, like, another state."

"*Very* far," Priya says.

"Um—" I say, but am instantly interrupted.

"Oh, another country then." Emily turns to Priya and acts all know-it-all. "Are you from India?"

Priya shakes her head.

"Pakistan?"

No again.

"Egypt?"

"Emily—"

Emily shuts me up with a raised hand. "Somalia?"

"Somalia? Jesus, Emily, no."

Priya herself interrupts us. "I'm from a planet—"

"Hey, how was Gran's?" I butt in. "You're back early."

"Near Gliese 581c," she finishes.

"Did you say—" Brian starts, but I cut him off too.

"Did Gran die or something?" I blurt out, earning me scowls from both of my friends.

"What?" Brian shakes his head. "Not cool, man, not cool."

Emily's stare burns a hole into me. She turns away, but this isn't the end. She's got a mystery to solve. The mystery of Priya.

Just then, the sweet scent of weed mixes with the smell of coconut suntan lotion. Brian holds a joint out to me but I wave my hand, no thanks. "Dude, did you check out that suit on Miranda? *Yasssssss*," he drawls. He's already forgotten that Priya thinks she's an alien space traveler. Thank god for his short attention span.

"Brian, hey, asshat? There're girls here." His sister punches him in the shoulder. "You wanna put it back in your shorts?"

"Whatever," Brian responds, exhaling a thin trail of smoke. "Like you're not checking out Eric."

Emily blushes. "I'm not."

"Oh my god, you so are."

"Screw you, Toad."

Brian jerks his thumb at his sister. "This is the brain trust going to Penn State?"

"Matthew, what are they doing?" Priya asks, seemingly

oblivious, thank god. She points a long arm at a group of kids racing to the raft.

"They're swimming," I say.

"Don't you know how to swim?" Em asks.

"Not everyone learned to swim when they were three, overachiever," her brother says.

"My god, stop arguing," I say. "Come on, Priya, let's go in the water."

I hold my hand to her and help her up. I recognize the wobble in her legs, the imminent buckling of her knees, and grab onto her waist before she can tumble—and before Brian and Em notice.

Brian doesn't.

Em does.

"She just said she doesn't know how to swim," Emily protests.

"Leave her alone," her brother mumbles as he pinches out the joint and tucks it into an Altoids tin.

"She didn't know the word, but she knows," I say. *Please, God or Universe or whatever, let me be right about this. For once, let me be right.*

"Where are *you* going?" I hear Emily ask Brian.

"None of your business" is Brian's mature retort.

"Better not be the lifeguard tower."

"Shut up, Em."

I take Priya by the hand and walk with her to the edge of the water.

Does she know how to swim? She has to know, right? I mean, everyone knows how to swim.

Her eyes meet mine. "I know how to swim," she says.

"Okay, but you're not wearing a bathing suit," I remind her. "You might not want to go too far."

We wade into the lake together and I feel Priya's hand grip mine tighter as the water laps at our feet. She jumps with each step.

"It's cold," she says.

But it's not. It's actually warm. Unusually warm.

Even so, she shivers and clings to me. I stand behind her and wrap my arms around her, keeping her warm, keeping her stable. There is barely any wind, but I worry that the slightest wave will knock her over.

Out of the corner of my eye, I see Brian approach the lifeguard tower. I can only imagine what he's saying to her, trying to get her attention:

Oh hey, Miranda, fancy meeting you here.

"This is beautiful," Priya says into my neck as she leans back into me. "I will miss this when I leave."

"No lakes where you're from?"

I feel her head shake. "Our water long ago stopped being entertainment. We experienced a drought that made us severely restrict water usage."

"Oh yeah, well, that happens." What does she mean? Where is she from? California, maybe? They've had a drought there for years. I wish she would just tell me the truth. Brian may not care, but Emily's the pit bull of the family. She won't let it go and she'll keep on me until she has an answer.

The sun on my shoulders heats up my T-shirt. I gotta take it off before I sweat to death. "I'm going to put this back on the sand, okay? I'll be right back."

I turn from her, stripping my shirt off over my head, and—

"What's wrong with her?" Emily asks me as soon as I turn toward the shore. She's standing on her towel, hands on her hips, surveying the lake like a sentry.

I brush past her, shoulder to shoulder, and go to my own towel. "I don't know what you're talking about."

"Matty, she's . . . different."

I snort. "Yeah, I know. That's what I like about her." I kneel on the towel and reach for the tote bag.

Emily stands over me, hovering behind my back, watching my every move, dissecting it.

"Matty."

"What."

"I mean, she's different, like, *different*. Like, *wrong*—"

I whip around and look up at Em. "There's nothing *wrong* with her. She's smart and she's sweet and she's interested in a lot of the same things I'm interested in."

Em holds my gaze. "She's super skinny."

I feel my eyes roll. "Oh, it's her weight. You're jealous."

"What? No!"

"Please, Em, I know what you're doing. It's like, fat-shaming or whatever." I wave a hand at her.

"I'm not jealous of her *weight*, for god's sake. You"—she punctuates the air with a finger—"are an idiot."

"Whatever. I'm an idiot." I start to go back to the lake but Emily stops me.

"If you can get past your ego for one second and the fact that I turned you down—"

"I don't care."

"And actually *listen* to what I'm saying—"

"What."

"Your girlfriend—"

"Not my girlfriend."

"—is like, *really* skinny. She doesn't look natural."

I shrug. "So, maybe she diets a lot."

"Or maybe she's sick. Or anorexic or something."

"Nope. I've seen her eat massive quantities of pizza. She loves pizza."

"Okay, bulimic then. She's sticking her finger down her throat when you're not looking."

Okay, *that's* gross. Girls are gross. "No, she's not."

"How do you know?"

"How do *you* know?"

"Hey, somebody help her!" We hear a kid behind us call out. Emily and I both turn and see Priya far away from shore, head barely above the water, hands waving, eyes bobbing, playing peekaboo with us. Definitely *not* swimming, not even kicking her legs in a doggy paddle.

"Hey!" I shout. "Priya, stop!"

"Miranda!" Emily yells at the lifeguard tower. "Eric!"

But Eric isn't there and Miranda is busy—with Brian, who is splashing in the water in front of her, feigning distress. "Brian, what the—"

When I turn, Emily is gone. In the time it takes me to look from the empty tower to Priya, Em is already in the lake, swimming toward the raft, her long arms pulling her through the water in fast, smooth strokes.

I feel panic constrict my throat and my stomach and I can't breathe, let alone shout for help. I hurl myself into the lake, flailing my arms and kicking my feet.

The sounds of the shore—the kids playing, the parents nagging, the lifeguard whistle blowing—become dulled background noise as I focus on Emily and Priya. It's as if I'm staring down a tunnel, and everything around me goes into dark, soft focus.

Ahead of me, Em's at Priya's side. She flips Priya upside down so she floats on her back, then scoots underneath. Hooking her arms underneath Priya's armpits, she swims backward, her powerful legs kicking and propelling them both to the shore. Emily is so much shorter than Priya, yet in the water, it's as if her body has elongated to ten feet, her arms like muscular tendrils around Priya's slender frame.

As they pass me, I hold on to Priya's legs and help speed Emily to shore. Together we lift her out of the lake and lower her gently to the sand, just out of the water's reach.

Miranda and Eric, the lifeguards who weren't guarding anyone's lives, suddenly appear out of the crowd. They quickly swoop in and edge Emily and me aside. Our eyes meet and I see the exhilaration in Emily's face, the satisfaction that she helped someone—*we* helped someone.

"Get back, everyone, back, back!" Eric commands the onlookers. I hold my ground, refusing to give up my spot in the sand. I need to make sure nothing happens, that she doesn't . . .

Oh my god. Please don't die.

Miranda does all the stuff she was taught in lifeguard class: she checks Priya's airways, listens to her breath with her head tilted sideways, feels for a pulse. Priya's chest very slowly rises and falls, her breath hiccupping a few times before becoming steady, if shallow. Miranda nods curtly but is obviously relieved. No one's dying on her watch. Not today, at least.

"She'll be fine," she says to the group of strangers. They sigh and applaud, belatedly. Eric and Miranda acknowledge the kudos even as they carefully move Priya from the sand to a blanket in the shade.

But everyone should be cheering for Emily's bravery, not these two clowns in Cheez-It suits. They didn't do anything remarkable. I search the onlookers for Emily, to thank her myself, but she's gone, faded into the crowd.

I hurry to Priya's side and kneel at the blanket. She's as still as if she were sleeping. I wipe water off her chin and eyes with the edge of a towel, careful not to get sand in them. Her long black lashes sparkle in the sunlight filtering through the leaves above. The chain around her neck threatens to strangle her; I carefully adjust the charm.

I call her name gently.

Her eyes flutter open and she looks panicked at first, then sees me. I feel her hand reach for mine. I squeeze back and don't let go.

"You said you could swim."

"I can," she says.

"No, you can't."

Her eyebrows knit. "I should be able to. I have the collected knowledge of thousands of people." She tries to sit up and coughs a couple of times, spitting up some of the brackish water she swallowed and wiping it away with the back of her hand. "I don't understand why I was unable to access that data." She appears truly perplexed. "I have done this before."

"You've gone swimming before?"

"No, but something similar. Back on my planet."

As she says this, I feel someone hovering behind me. I glance over my shoulder and see Emily. She holds a bottle of water with a straw in it.

She heard. Every word.

"Um, for, uh . . . her. She should take slow sips," she says. Then addressing Priya directly, she adds, "Don't gulp it down, okay?"

Priya takes the water and nods. "Thank you. You saved me."

Emily looks away, embarrassed. "Oh, um, yeah, okay." Her gaze meets mine. "Matty, can I talk to you? Over there?" She jerks her head toward the water.

I follow Em to the edge of the lake, far enough away that Priya can't hear us but not so far that I can't keep an eye on her. I don't want to let her out of my sight.

"What's going on?" Emily's tone is blunt.

"You asked me that already. I told you. She's visiting from out of town."

"*Way* out of town, to hear her talk." Em crosses her arms over her chest. "Is she, like, slow or something?"

"Slow? What are you—"

"Is she an escaped mental patient?"

"N-noooo?" I answer less quickly. Emily notices my split-second hesitation and seizes upon it.

"Have you checked her ID?"

"Why would I—"

"Have you checked her phone?"

"She doesn't have one."

"Everyone has a phone."

"She doesn't."

"Well, that's not normal, either."

"Just because she doesn't have a phone—"

"And she thinks she's from another planet."

"—doesn't mean she has *mental issues*. She's sweet and kind and, you know, totally harmless, so what's the big fucking deal?"

Emily takes me by the shoulders. Her hands are cool, her skin moist. "Matty, she's wearing a white wig on top of her hair."

"Duh. I know that."

"Yeah, okay, but—"

"Girls wear wigs, Em. It's not a sign of mental instability."

We both look over at Priya sitting on the blanket. As usual, her legs are stretched out in front of her, two long sticks under a wilted tutu. She doesn't see us watching her as she struggles to aim her mouth around the straw.

I hear Emily's voice as I watch Priya. "Look, Matty . . . when I was in the water with her, I noticed the wig slip off. And . . ." Em pauses.

"And . . . go on."

"She has a scar, like, a really crazy scar here." Em draws a finger from the side of her head down to the base of her hairline in the shape of a C.

"So?" I shrug her off even though, yeah, of course it's weird and of course I care. A scar like that could mean a lot of things. However, none of those things are any of Emily's business.

"She's covering something up."

"If you had a scar like that, you'd cover it up too."

Em shakes her own ponytail; wet like a rag, it smacks against her back and neck. "That's not what I mean. Maybe you should talk to your mom about her. She's a nurse. She might know something that—"

"I don't need to talk to my mother. I don't need to talk to anyone."

I see Brian shuffling over to Priya, dropping his butt onto the towel next to her. He holds a joint out to her. I wonder if I should intervene. Do they have pot on her planet?

Did I just . . . ?

"Maybe she's from another country, all right? Maybe English isn't her first language."

"Fine." She pounces. "What is?"

"I have no idea, Em." And that is the absolute truth. "But look, she's not going to be here for very long and I really want to hang out with her." I keep my gaze steady on Em until she nods that she gets it.

"Yeah, sure. I just think maybe you should allow for the idea that while hanging out with her and pretending everything's okay is good for *you*—it might not be good for *her.*"

There is a long pause after she says this, and I feel like something more is coming, there's something more she wants to say, but she doesn't. "We cool?"

Em sighs heavily. "Whatever, dipshit."

I start to walk away and then stop. "Thanks for . . . you

know." I know she knows what I mean: *Thanks for saving Priya's life.*

"Yeah, yeah. Just don't let her smoke any of that crap Brian's got."

"No good?" Em rarely smokes, but she knows quality.

She shakes her head. "It smells like a pizza."

"Huh. She might like that, actually."

I get to Priya just as Brian is showing her how to inhale.

"She doesn't smoke," I say, pushing the joint away from her. "And that's not even good shit. Em says it's, like, oregano or something."

Brian brings the burning end of the joint right up to his eye. "What?" He holds it up to me. "Try it yourself."

"No. And by the way, fuck you," I tell him. I start to gather our stuff and shove it all in the canvas tote.

"What? Fuck me? Why?"

"You were talking to Miranda, distracting her from watching the lake. Priya could have drowned."

My friend's mouth opens and closes. "But . . . but . . . Em was there."

"What if she wasn't?"

"But she *was*."

I help Priya up and tug her along with me. If Toad says anything of substance after that—which is doubtful—I don't hear it.

4:17 P.M.

Emily's questions haunt me on the ride home. With every twist on the road, every dip and turn we take, I feel Priya's fingers grip my shirt and press into my skin and I think:

What is wrong with you?

Where are you from?

Who are you, really?

Why won't you tell me the truth?

I'm silent as I pull the bike into the garage, quiet as I put away towels and shake the sand out of my sneakers. Priya looks tired, even as she stoops to greet Ginger, who only has eyes for the girl, whose tail swishes happily on the grass. My dog isn't particularly discerning when it comes

EIGHT DAYS ON PLANET EARTH

to humans. If they have food or a hand to pet her, she's over the moon. But can she detect good character?

Can I?

What, I wonder, will make Priya crack? What will be the thing that makes her break down and tell me the truth?

And then it hits me. I have it.

4:30 P.M.

We have the World's Oldest VCR.

It's the only thing I can use to play the video of "our" episode of *Real-Life Mystery*, a reality show from the early nineties that hardly anyone watched about things that never really happened. In this case, it's the UFO landing in the space field. The show chose our small town and our small UFO event since it was the twenty-fifth anniversary of the supposed crash landing.

(And not for nothing, but if aliens have the kind of technology to travel light-years across the galaxy, don't you think they could have avoided crashing into Earth? I mean, it's right *there*. They would have *seen* it. Whatever.)

I clear some space on the living room couch for Priya to sit and turn on all the doodads to get the VCR going. She settles into the cushions eagerly, her eyes alight with anticipation.

I sit next to her and press play on the remote. There's a loud hum as the machine whirs to life.

The tape has been played so many times, paused and examined frame by frame, that there are actual ridges in it. The audio clicks and pops as the damaged tape passes over the metal heads inside the machine. I have to crank the volume way up to get any decent sound out of it.

". . . tonight we reveal the truth behind the aliens next door." The voice-over guy hits the words *truth* and *aliens* megahard, in case you don't get it. *This is gonna be some serious shit, people, brace yourselves.*

The screen dissolves from its opening title to a shot of a sky filled with stars.

"This is, like, we're the aliens, you know. We're floating in space," I tell Priya. "Oh, and that's a map of Pennsylvania so you can see where in the whole state our crappy little town is."

Cut back to space and now we're moving faster, plummeting through the atmosphere toward Earth. "These are, like, the lamest special effects ever. Like, ever. How much did they spend on this, ten bucks?"

I feel Priya's gaze on me but she says nothing. I'm sure she's engrossed in the spectacularity that is *Real-Life Mystery*.

"It's not like it's in a suburb of McMansions. I mean, it's just some crummy field and no one even died. And it was empty, too. It was the middle of winter and my granddad didn't even have anything growing."

The camera swoops down into the field as if it were on a helicopter, trying hard to make us feel like we're "in" the ship.

And then a smash cut to black as we "hit" the ground, fade up to a shot of fog surrounding a cone-shaped metal object. "That is so clearly a model . . . ," I mumble. I can't help myself.

For the next half hour, though, even fast-forwarding through the commercials for *Joe Versus the Volcano*, I try to stay silent to allow Priya to absorb the whole fiasco. The docudrama *is* absorbing in a train wreck sort of way. I've seen it so many times, I've memorized every scene, every hint of conspiracy, every interview—including the one with DJ Jones.

Throughout, I half watch the screen, half watch Priya. She's impassive, her beautiful face a blank. I can't tell if she thinks this is silly or stupendous.

"Well?" I ask when the credits finally roll. I hit pause on the remote.

"Remarkable," she says. "This is not true, of course."

I exhale, relieved beyond belief. "Thank you. No, not at all."

She points at the freeze-frame on screen, which is a shot of the crashed ship under the credits. "There are so many questions left unanswered." She begins ticking off points on her long fingers. "What technology brought that ship here? Did its designers have faster-than-light propulsion? If so, what was the matter used to create it?"

"Um . . ."

"Or did it travel through a wormhole? If so, which one? From where? Why didn't it disintegrate upon entering Earth's atmosphere?"

"Well, I—"

"When it was experiencing problems, why didn't its pilots seek the water, which is, actually, the majority of the surface of this planet and easier to survive?"

"Uh, yeah—"

She mutters, as if to herself. "A wormhole is the more likely of the two options since faster-than-light travel, as it is currently understood, requires a warp bubble that allows the contraction of space ahead of the vehicle and the expansion of it behind. A stable warp bubble is nearly impossible to create, while a stable wormhole is, at least, viable at this time."

She stops and looks at me, expecting me to . . . chime in? I only know half of the words she just said. They were English, right?

"But it's not real," I say. "None of it. There was no crash. There was no ship. There was no government cover-up."

She falls back into the cushion, her thin frame sinking into the fabric. Her gaze on me does not even acknowledge what I just said. "Not to mention the pilots themselves. Where are they? Why didn't a second ship rescue them?" Her lip quivers. "Would they have simply been *left* here to be captured? To be held prisoner?"

"But it's—"

She turns to me, her gaze intense and withering. "Not real, so you said. But it *is* real. That field *was* the site of a crash landing. I can feel it when I'm there. And you can too, even if you insist you can't."

"Priya, you just said there were so many unanswered questions," I try to reason with her. "The landing, the method of travel—"

"I don't need answers."

"Well, *I* do."

"That is *your* problem."

I can feel my temperature rise, and not in a good way at all. "Look, it wasn't even produced very well. The aliens were just really tall people in metallic sweat suits and they carried plastic weapons." I force a laugh, but she won't be swayed.

"They talked to people who were there, Matthew. They—"

"They were idiots!" I shout. "Complete lunatics!"

Her eyes grow wide and she lurches to a standing position, fists on hips even as she nearly topples over. "Do you not understand? Each day I'm here, I am *not* at my home. You are here! You are home."

You are here. An image of space pops into my head, an array of planets against a field of stars, and a red arrow aimed squarely at a speck on the Big Blue Marble. Me. Home. This is my home. Why isn't it Priya's? Or more important, why doesn't she think it is?

I take her by the shoulders and force her to look at me. "Priya, you are *not* an alien. You are a girl, a human. Please, *please*, tell me who you are and where you're from so I can help you."

"Matthew—"

She tries to pull away, but I hold fast. "You're not home and I want to help you *get* home, but it's not going to be in a fucking spaceship! Okay? Listen to me!"

"No! Listen to *me*! I am what I say I am—what you *know* I am."

I keep her gaze, and for the first time, I see her as Emily saw her: white wig askew, dark circles like bruises around her eyes, her breath shallow and fast.

"No, I don't know what you are."

Her eyes fly open. "You do!"

"I just want you to be—"

She wrenches free of me and stomps out of the living room, the heels of her boots clicking on the floor, with

Ginger as her shadow. At the kitchen door, she fumbles with the lock. As I come up behind her, I see her fingers slip over and over again, like they're unable to grasp the knob and turn it. She's so angry with me that she can't focus. She struggles with the door, grunting as she pushes and pulls the handle, trying to yank it and shove it and slam her hands against it in frustration.

Normal. I just want you to be normal.

I wait until she gives up and leans her shoulder against the wall. Gently, very gently, I wrap my hand around hers and unlock the door with her. I feel her fingers trembling from the effort before they free themselves from my grasp.

As soon as I open the door, she escapes, just like Ginger does, without a glance backward, anxious to be free of the confines of my house.

I watch as she gallops, colt-like, through the willows, the branches trailing down her back like hair, emerging on the other side, tripping up the gentle slope toward the field.

She stands, dead center of the field, alone, arms slack by her sides. Her head falls back and her face lifts. I can imagine her smile from here. Is that where she is happiest? In the magical space field? Where she can somehow feel the energy of a long-ago crash?

I hear Ginger whine at my feet. I'm standing in the doorway, blocking her path.

I step aside and she escapes as Priya did, charging up the hill.

Normal. *Why can't you be a normal girl?*

She's so desperate to be out there, out in that stupid field. Desperate to hitch a ride on a comet or a rocket to the moon.

Fine, let her stay there.

I close the door, lock it.

7:31 P.M.

After two hours of dying and respawning in Halo and trying to forget the argument I had with Priya, I shut off my
Xbox and drag my butt downstairs to find my mother in the
kitchen. "When did you get home?"

She's in sweats, changed from her work scrubs, and her
hair is wet. "Not long ago. You upstairs?"

"Yeah."

"Anyone with you?"

"Um, no. . . ."

Why would she ask that? Does she know about Priya?
Did she see her in the field? My heart begins to pound and I
force myself to take deep breaths.

Okay, Matty, tell her. Do it.

I have to do this. I have to ask Mom about Priya. I have to get her help, even though Priya will probably hate me for it, even if Mom blasts me for keeping her a secret.

"So, Mom, I—"

And then I notice she's got her laptop on the table and an intense, troubled look on her face. The computer is an old Dell that Dad and I refurbished for her about a million years ago. I think she mostly uses it as a paperweight. "What's that?"

"The blog," she tells me. "His blog." Her voice trembles and her finger shakes as she points at the screen.

"What about it?"

"It's been updated." She sits back and turns the screen toward me.

It's a selfie of my dad in front of a nondescript city building. His shaggy sand-colored hair is blowing back in a wind and the too-close camera distorts his nose and chin, making him look like Ginger when she sniffs the phone.

"Read it," my mother commands.

It's brief, just a few lines of that god-awful white text on a black background, but the key words I see are: *It's the start of a new adventure.*

I scan the rest of the entry but the words blur. I shove the laptop back at my mom. "Whatever. So he's telling the world he's gone. So what? We knew that. Now everyone else knows it too."

But that's not enough for my mom. She picks up the computer and follows me to the sink, where I'm running the water for a glass. She thrusts the screen at me again. "Where is he? Can you tell?"

"No."

"Look, Matty. Please."

"Fine." I stare again at his photo. Behind him is a stone building, gray with round columns. There's a blue-and-white bus in one corner and a tree in the other. "A city, I guess."

"But *where*?"

Where in the world is David James Jones?

"I still can't believe he hasn't contacted us," my mother says, nibbling on one nail.

Uhhh . . .

I can't tell her. I need her to let this go, let him go. I want to remind her that he left with another woman, but that would be cruel. *Face facts, Lorna.*

"Not even a call?"

When she says "call," the phone number Dad gave me suddenly pops into my brain.

Stupid brain, why are you remembering that, *of all things?* I can't seem to remember enough to pass English lit, but I can remember a group of ten numbers *I don't want to know*?

2. 6. 7.

267.

Two six seven. I do a quick Google search on Mom's laptop and come up with the answer: Philadelphia. My heart blips a beat. He's actually just a four-hour drive away.

That's it? That's where he went?

I guess I'd imagined Dad heading for L.A., the sun on his face, salt spray in his hair, with Carol by his side in a shiny red convertible. I have no idea why I would picture this, since my dad drives a pickup truck and his fair skin burns the moment he steps outside.

Knowing he's in the same state as me is both reassuring and disappointing.

"Is it Hollywood?" my mom asks.

Lie or truth? Which will hurt my mother more? If she knows he's close by, will she flip out and go there herself? I answer my question and hers at the same time. "Yeah, probably."

Oh god, this is killing me. I don't *want* to know more than my mom. I kind of just want to be a dumb kid. That's what she expects, right? What everyone expects?

My mother stands behind me and begins to massage my shoulders. "It's okay, Matty. We'll be okay, you and me." She kisses me on the top of my head, something she hasn't done since I was a baby, probably, the last time I was shorter than her. "I'm going to cook dinner for us."

"You are?"

"Why are you so shocked?"

I turn in my chair to watch her start the motions of cooking a meal. "Is your name Colonel Sanders? Or Marie Callender?"

"It's Olive Garden, actually. Didn't you know that?"

"Oh, you're famous!"

"I am. And cheap."

"Two things I admire most in a person," I say.

My mother grins and holds up a frying pan. "Okay, tonight we'll be serving chicken."

"We will? And where will we be getting chicken?" My mom is nearly clueless in this kitchen. She has no idea that we don't have any ingredients besides coffee and mashed potatoes. I start to get up but she waves the pan at me.

"Sit down. I'm doing this tonight."

"You really are? I need to write this down in my diary."

She somehow manages to hold the pan *and* give me the finger.

I give it right back. "Bring it on, Ms. Garden. I'll take two of everything."

Mom grins, which brings a smile to my face too. I like seeing her happy. I like being cooked for, although I'm glad we have pizza on speed-dial. We might need to place an order when she realizes we have no actual food with which to make an actual dinner.

"Matty, did you need something from me?"

"Huh?"

"When you came in? You seemed like you wanted to talk

about something. I'm sure it wasn't your dad and his blog."
She rolls her eyes like I do, which makes me laugh.

I hesitate for a fraction of a second. Now is the time
to take Em's advice and get Mom's professional opinion.
Maybe it will be okay.

But then . . .

. . . I hear Mom hum.

God, she's happy. For once, finally, she's happy. I shake
my head. "It can wait. I'm pretty hungry."

My mother waves a spatula at me like it's a wand. "You
got it."

After dinner. I promise I'll ask her after dinner.

DAY SEVEN

7:01 A.M.

I ate too much pizza.

Yeah, that meal wasn't my mom's finest effort. She did the best she could with what she had, but honestly, no. It was crap. The pizza, on the other hand, was amazing. I scarfed six of the eight slices along with a side of garlic knots and brownie bites.

And then I fell asleep on the couch as Mom and I watched a movie on Netflix.

I awake alone, though, and the television is off. Mom must have crawled up to her room, leaving me to sleep down here.

I stumble to the kitchen to start the coffee, start my

day, when I remember I locked the door. If Priya needed to use the bathroom or the phone or just to come inside, she wouldn't have been able to.

Stupid, Matty. Stupid.

The sun is creeping up over the horizon as I head out to the field barefoot. It feels good to touch the earth with my toes, to sink my heels into the dewy grass. The slender blades spring back into place with each step I take.

I blink a few times when I get to the field.

I don't see Priya.

Turning in a circle, I search the field and the surrounding woods for her. Is she curled up with Ginger somewhere? But I don't see the dog either.

Telescope.

Tent.

No girl. No dog.

I peel the tent flap back. "Priya? Are you—"

Ginger is lying in the middle of the tent, her tail wrapped around her, her paws crossed with her chin resting atop them. I'm overwhelmed with a feeling of déjà vu.

The garage. Empty. And now this.

My stomach sinks to my feet. "She's gone," I tell Ginger, who obviously knows. She drags herself to me and rests her head under my hand, nudging it for a pet, as if rubbing my palm over her silky ears will make everything better.

It does, but not for very long.

I can't believe it. One night—one goddamn night—that I'm not out here with her, and she leaves. I shake my head when I feel tears cloud my eyes.

I knew she had to go at some point. I knew she couldn't live in this field forever.

"But . . ."

The telescope is still aimed at the sky, at that distant spot in the Universe that called to Priya. During the day, I won't be able to see anything, but I look through it anyway, careful to avoid pointing it directly at the sun.

She's just a girl. She's not an alien.

My heart plummets. I know. I knew. I did. But . . .

I want to believe. I need to believe.

In something. In someone.

I bend down to Ginger and let her lick my face and nuzzle her cold nose under my chin. "Where did she go, girl? Did she tell you?"

My dog's brown eyes look worried, or maybe I'm just projecting.

And maybe she's not really gone. Maybe she's out for a walk or she slept under the trees. Maybe the sneaky girl is actually in my house somewhere, having discovered a way into the basement or attic, and maybe if I wait, she'll come back.

But as the minutes pass and she doesn't walk out of the woods after a quick pee and she doesn't amble up the hill from the workshop, the realization that she is really and truly gone finally sinks in, settling into my bones like a frigid wind.

Where the hell is she?

Did she walk away? Drive away? Call a taxi or an Uber? Did her boyfriend or family find her? My head swirls with the possibilities.

I pace the field as if it would tell me something, give me a clue. My bare feet stumble over dry branches and rocks and leaves.

She's gone. She's really gone.

But where? I start to head down to the house, and in my mind, I've hopped on my bike and begun to cruise the streets of my crappy town to see if she's wandering around. Maybe she went to the DQ to talk to a tree? To the lake for a swim? To the Aokis' to visit Felicette?

I call to Ginger but she doesn't budge. I clap my hands. "Come on, girl!"

Normally I wouldn't care. Normally I don't give a shit if the dog wants to stay up here and bake in the sun. But this week has been anything but normal and I do care. I take a few menacing steps closer to Ginger, growling at her, and still she holds her ground.

Next to the telescope.

Which has a white paper tied around a tripod leg.

What on earth?

It's not paper, though, it's nylon, and as soon as I bend

down to peer closer at it, I recognize what it is instantly because I've seen a million of them: a hospital ID bracelet. My heart thumps as I carefully unwrap it from the tripod. It's definitely a bracelet, but the part where it was tied around the stand is shredded and the words are indistinct.

Shah, Priya

Johnson, Simone MD

DOB 2/12/00

There's one line—the most important one, damn it—that isn't clear. Where it should say the name of the hospital, all I can read is *PHILA*.

Priya has a last name. And a date of birth. And a doctor. And a hospital that's probably in Philadelphia.

I hear Em's voice in my head: *Maybe she's sick.*

Too skinny. Too clumsy. Too . . . scarred.

She's not crazy. She's not a mental patient. She's not . . . an alien.

Em's voice again: *Maybe you should talk to your mom.*

I didn't! Why didn't I? Oh god.

I clutch the bracelet in my fist and run all the way to the house, jumping over the stream and nearly tripping in the grass. If anyone knows about hospitals, it's my mother, the nurse.

"Mom! Mom! Are you up?" I charge up the stairs. Bedroom's empty, bathroom's empty.

And back down. Not in the kitchen or the laundry room.

"Mom!"

Her purse and keys and cell are missing from their usual spots.

So is her car.

"Are you serious?" My voice echoes in the garage. Ginger sits at my feet, ever patient.

I'm always—*always*—a step behind. I never seem to think ahead, to anticipate the possibilities of things to come. I never saw Emily's rejection, or my dad taking off, or Priya's sickness. That's what it is, right? God, how dumb can one person be?

Will it always be this way? Will I always be left in the dust of the empty garage, the vacant field? Will I always be blindsided and crushed?

"I can't let her go," I tell Ginger. "I can't. I have to find her."

I open my hand and unfurl the bracelet: *Shah, Priya*.

"Let's start with that."

7:45 A.M.

When I do a search for "Priya Shah" and "Philadelphia," I come up with dozens of hits. The first few are news sites with headlines like "Local girl missing," and subheads such as, "Teen leaves hospital; public urged to contact authorities."

"Teen" is Priya Shah, a patient who slipped out of her room at a children's hospital in Philadelphia in the middle of the night shortly after a nurse checked on her. According to the brief articles, her parents have been worried sick since she disappeared. Their only daughter. Their only child.

I suck in my breath when I see the photo of her that

accompanies the article. It must be from middle school or junior high. Priya's face is fuller, her cheeks round and plump, and her hair is thick, silky, black. If it weren't for her deep-set eyes, grinning at the photographer taking her picture, I would think this wasn't Priya at all but her younger, healthier sister.

No wonder no one found her, if they thought *that* was the girl they were looking for.

I scan more articles, but they're all old and only minimally helpful. There's a Facebook page someone set up for the Shahs with plenty of good wishes for them and loads of false leads.

I saw her get on a plane to Florida.

She was in the bar I was at last night.

She's in NYC! Times Square!

But then they stopped after a couple of days; no doubt some other missing girl took the spotlight and Priya's parents were left on their own.

And now?

The ID bracelet has to be her clue for me. It has to be. She must have left it for me to find—to find *her.* I get the number for the hospital and dial it, stabbing button after button to get to the patient information desk.

"Uh, hi, yeah, I'm trying to find out if my girlfriend has been admitted to the hospital."

"Name?"

"My name is Matthew Jones."

The man on the other end laughs. "No, sir, the patient's name."

In a fevered rush, I blurt out all of the information on the bracelet: Priya's full name and birth date, her doctor's name. I even describe exactly what she looks like and what she was wearing the last time I saw her and I tell him I know she was missing for six days but all that time she was staying with me and now she's gone and I—

"Yes, sir, Miss Shah is our patient."

Relief washes over me. I knew it was a clue. I just knew it. She *wants* me to find her.

Philadelphia, however, is over four hours away and there is no way my dirt bike is going to make it. I need a car.

Emily answers on the first ring. "Now *you're* calling *me*."

"Em, I need your car."

"Excuse me?"

I run up to my room, juggling the phone while I change shirts, jeans, socks and—what the hell—underwear, too. "Priya's gone and it's all my fault. She's in Philly and my bike is not exactly street legal. I need to borrow your car."

"Slow down. Tell me what's going on."

I take a breath and explain the whole story. It's as messy as my call to the hospital, but I don't care.

"Why is it your fault?" Em asks.

I run a hand through my hair and over my whiskers. Time to shave? "I don't want to talk about it."

"No talk, no car."

"Fine, whatever, okay. I pushed her, all right? I made fun of her for thinking she was . . ."

"An alien?" Em prompts.

I feel heat rise in my chest and my pulse quickens. "I was such an idiot. I basically told her she was a lunatic."

"You didn't say 'lunatic.'"

"I didn't say 'lunatic' but I . . . strongly hinted at it." I kick the pile of clothes on the floor until I find a pair of Nikes. "Em, I treated her like crap. And I . . . I just left her."

Silence on the other end of the phone, only Emily's slow breathing, and then she says, "I'll drive."

I start to argue, but she's already hung up.

10:41 A.M.

Stopping only for coffee and gas, we stick to the turnpike and head east to Philly. Emily is on a mission, eyes on the road, hands at ten and two on the wheel of her Jeep. Brian's sleeping in the backseat, one leg slung over the spare tire. I didn't ask him to join us, but Em insisted.

We come to a toll booth about an hour outside Philly and there's a long line of cars waiting in the cash-only line. The sun is like a hammer on my head through the open roof.

We've been driving in silence and fearsome concentration for almost three hours. Finally, Em speaks.

"It's my fault," she says. "Not yours."

I blink. "Huh?"

"At the lake, I made it sound like there was something wrong with her—"

"There was. There is."

"I pushed you to find out, to confront her. If I hadn't said those things, maybe . . ."

"Maybe what?"

"Maybe she wouldn't have left by herself. Maybe you'd be with her now." Her voice is so quiet, I can barely hear her over the engines idling around us.

"Maybe," I say.

Em jerks the Jeep forward and holds her hand out to me. "Money, please."

I give her a ten and she pockets the change.

12:27 P.M.

In Philadelphia, I give Em turn-by-turn directions to get us to the hospital. Imposing and sterile-looking with lots of windows and a water fountain in the front. It looks secure, and I wonder how Priya managed to escape from it undetected.

Ah, but she's stealthy. After all, she spent a day in my house and in Dad's workshop without me or my mother even knowing she was there, and she knew exactly how to sneak around the Aokis' house looking for Boo. I imagine her slipping out of the hospital via a back staircase, hiding whenever someone happened by. She was determined to get to that field for some reason, and I have no doubt she could have awkwardly scaled the outside of this building, if that was what it took, with no one batting an eye.

"This is it," I tell Em, banging a hand on the dashboard. She finds the parking garage and locates a spot close to the stairs.

"You coming in?" I ask her.

"You sure you want me?"

I point at Brian, who's still asleep. "Him? No. You? Yes."

"He can be supportive, you know, when you give him a chance." She frowns. "I can't believe I'm saying that."

"Yeah. No."

She hesitates for a moment and then tucks her keys into Brian's pocket. "Okay. I'm sure he'll be fine."

My palms begin to sweat on the walk. I turn to Emily. "Thank you for doing this."

"What else was I going to do today?"

"I don't know. Swim, probably."

"Yeah, probably."

"Look, Em . . . I know she's just—"

"Go," she commands. "Just go."

Because of my mom, I've been in hospitals often enough to know that being kind and polite goes a lot further than making demands on staff. At the information desk I show the receptionist Priya's ID bracelet and ask if it's at all possible that I, and my very respectful friend here, could see our friend.

"I'll send you up," she says. "But it's the parents' say-so if you can go in."

On the way up in the elevator, I start to sweat again. Since I discovered Priya was missing this morning, I haven't even stopped to consider what might be wrong with her. The news articles were brief and didn't mention anything about her illness.

Does she have a virus? An infection? A disease?

Is she on the mend? In the middle of some kind of treatment? Or . . .

Ding! The elevator stops on our floor but I can't move. Emily takes my arm and pulls me out. "It's okay, Matty. I'm with you."

They tried to make this floor festive: the doctors and nurses are wearing purples and pinks and funky sneakers; there are stripes on the floors and murals on the walls. But they can't disguise the smell. The disinfectant in a hospital is like no other. They must all buy it from the same company.

The woman who opens Priya's door is clearly her mother. She has the same bright eyes and sharp cheekbones, the same arched eyebrows and dimpled upper lip, even the same diamond stud in her nose. But what she doesn't have is Priya's narrow frame. This woman is heavier by about forty pounds, what I imagine Priya will look like when she's middle-aged.

"May I help you?" she asks, not unkindly, but I can tell she'd have no problem kicking us to the curb if we don't provide the right answer.

"I'm, um, a, um, friend of Priya's," I say. "Matty, um, Matthew Jones."

Emily hurriedly introduces herself with a handshake. "Emily Aoki."

Priya's mother cocks her head to one side and considers us. "Priya knows you?"

"Um, she was um, staying? Yeah, she was staying in the field next to my house. I, um, I found this there." I pull out the ID bracelet and hand it to her. Realization dawns on her face and she nods, finally.

"I'm Priya's mother, Dr. Anisha Shah."

I wait, but no invitation seems to be forthcoming. "So, um, can I see her?" I ask. "Just to say hi. And bye," I add quickly.

"Her father is in with her now," she replies.

I look over at Emily, who encourages me with a bob of her head. "We won't stay long, Dr. Shah, but since we drove all this way, could we spend a minute or two with her?"

As Dr. Shah inspects each of us for an ulterior motive, my brain is fighting to wrap itself around this new reality of Priya Shah and whatever it was I saw over the past few days. Why would a person run away from a hospital and pretend to be an alien waiting for a ride back to her planet?

I just don't get it.

Eventually, Dr. Shah steps aside and lets us into Priya's room. My breath catches when I see her lying there, white sheet up to her armpits, her wig gone. Wispy black strands of hair swirl around her head like cotton candy. Beside her in a chair is her father, dressed in a shirt and tie and shiny brown loafers, both elbows on her bed. He barely glances at us when we walk in.

"Priya, love, your friends are here," Dr. Shah says. Her eyes well up and she wipes away a tear with the tip of one finger.

While I approach the bed, I hear Emily say quietly, "Matty was really worried about her, Dr. Shah. He took care of her, you know, while she was in the field and I know he made sure she had food and a place to sleep. He's a really good guy. . . ."

If there is more, I don't hear it. I focus all my attention on Priya, whose eyes are still closed.

"Rohan Shah," her father says to me, holding out his hand.

"Matty Jones," I say, trying to be Mr. Respectable when all I want to do is swallow Priya up whole.

"Thank you for watching over her."

"Well, I didn't really, you know, uh, no problem," I babble stupidly.

Her father gently shakes her awake.

"Hmmm?"

"Hi, Priya," I say, and she sees me then. For a brief,

tense moment I wonder if she is still angry with me, but then her face splits into a huge grin.

"Matthew!"

I hear Dr. Shah sigh, relieved I am who I say I am.

"Priya, I'm so . . . I can't . . ." I lean closer to Priya but I can't touch her, can't kiss her—not with her parents and Emily here. My heart skips when I see the C-shaped scar on the side of her head. *Oh god, how did I not know?*

"I didn't want to leave you," she says. "I'm sorry."

"No, I'm sorry. I got . . . distracted."

Behind me I hear Emily ask a question of Priya's parents, drawing them aside so I can talk with Priya on my own. I thank her silently.

"How is my dog?" Priya asks. "Is she eating well?"

My dog . . . my heart skips. I wish I'd brought Ginger with me, although they never would have let me in with her. I nod up and down, reassuringly. "She's great, really good."

I think of the ID bracelet around the tripod. "She helped me find you."

"She is a very smart dog. I was not allowed to bring her with me, although she tried to accompany me."

". . . anaplastic astrocytomas . . . ," I hear Dr. Shah say in the silence.

Emily whispers another question and Priya's mother replies, "Surgery and radiation . . ."

Priya pushes herself up on her elbows. "Thank you for retrieving me. I'm ready to return to the field."

"Oh, um, I don't think you can go."

"What? Why not?"

"Because . . . well . . . you're here now."

"This is . . ." She blinks a few times, searching for the word. "Not a permanent state? What do I mean?"

"Temporary?"

"Yes. A temporary state. I can go now."

"But—"

"Isn't that why you came here? To bring me back to the field?"

"Well, no, I—"

Priya clutches at me. "Matthew, what will I do? How will I get home?" Her eyes narrow with worry and her lips quiver. I feel her cold fingers on my arm and I long to warm her up, to hold her in my arms and never let her go.

"Maybe you should stay here," I suggest. "Just for a little while."

"No, no. I need to go back to the field. You must bring me back there with you."

I glance over my shoulder at Dr. Shah and Emily, still whispering. "It's not that simple—"

"Yes, of course it is! It's very simple!" She starts to sit up but collapses nearly instantly.

I don't care if her parents are here, if Emily is watching. I wrap my arms around Priya and hold her; I feel her hands at my waist and her cheek against my neck. A sob grabs the back of my throat.

The look in her eyes, pleading. I know what it means. *Help.* She needs my help.

What are you going to do, Matty? Kidnap her?

My gaze sweeps the room. It feels empty, I notice, not like other hospital rooms, and I realize for the first time what's missing: the hum of machines. It's not like what you'd expect to see, what they show on TV and in movies. It's more like a room at home, the walls painted a buttery yellow, real curtains over the window, and an actual lamp with a shade beside the bed.

Even if I managed to sneak her out from under her parents' very sharp gaze, what would we gain? Another night in the middle of the field, waiting to be picked up by an alien rocket ship?

"Matthew, my head hurts," she says suddenly, pushing me away. Her fingers grab her head and push against her skull. "I don't want to stay here!" She flails at me, swinging her long arms.

I feel so useless. I just sit here, dumb, not understanding. I can't help. I can't do anything useful.

"Matthew, I think you should leave now," Priya's mother says as she and her husband move to subdue Priya. Although she flaps her arms and kicks at them, they don't stop comforting her, don't stop taking care of her. Her father coos to her, offering soothing words even as she resists him.

I'm watching a complete breakdown. The crazy-beautiful girl I love is falling apart in front of my eyes and I can't help her.

Helpless. Useless. *Why can't I ever do anything?*

For a split second, Priya and I lock eyes, and I see in hers . . . fear and accusation. I betrayed her. I abandoned her.

As she lifts her face toward the ceiling and lets out a horrific cry, I feel Emily slip her hand into mine. I grip it so tightly that I might break her fingers as she leads me out of the room.

4:01 P.M.

"That's it? That's how you left?" Brian asks me when Em hits the road for home.

I wrap my hands around a cup of crappy coffee we picked up at the hospital cafeteria before we left. "What else was I supposed to do?"

"But she needed you," he says.

"What do you know? You weren't there. And you don't even know her." I throw him a side eye. He hasn't even noticed that I'm pissed at him. Or if he has, he hasn't said anything.

"Toad, go back to sleep," Emily says. "Smoke a joint or something."

"First of all, I don't have any weed, and second of all . . ." He raises a weak middle finger to the rearview mirror.

Em lifts her coffee in response. "Nice."

"I just wish I could have done more for her," I say, ignoring them both.

"Matty, what could you have done?" Em wants to know. "She needed help. Real help. Medical help."

"My mom is a nurse," I say. That sounds lame. "You told me to talk to her and I never did."

"It doesn't matter. She still would have needed to be here. Would've needed her meds or whatever."

I don't mention the absence of meds and other hospital equipment in Priya's room. Apparently Emily didn't notice.

"She's comfortable now," Em says. "Did you see how nice her room was? The prettiest hospital room I've ever seen."

"Yeah."

"She's sick, Matty."

"But I didn't *know* she was sick. I thought she was . . ."

I don't know what I believed. I believed what she believed because I wanted to believe in *her*, whoever she was, wherever she was from.

We drive in silence for a minute, then five, then ten.

I let my head fall back and look up at the sky. The sun moves in and out of the clouds and the air feels moist on my skin.

Brian pokes his head around my shoulder, his wide back

blocking out Emily. "I know you're pissed, dude. I get it."

"Whatever." I don't want to talk about this now. Not now.

"And I know you don't really care what I think."

"Toad—"

"But I just think . . . I just think you were the one who was supposed to help her."

I let my head turn to Brian and meet his gaze. "What do you mean?"

"Her parents, well, they don't sound like they *got her*, you know? Like, you . . . got her."

She got me is more like it.

He takes my silence as agreement or at least permission and gets more confident as he goes on. "She came to the space field—"

"It's just a field," Em interjects.

"And found you. And you understand all that stuff. All the science and everything. . . . Her parents just brought her back to the hospital," he says. "They didn't care that the field was important to her. Not like you did."

Did I?

Brian shrugs and sits back in his seat. "Just sayin'."

I glance back at my friend who has his feet up on the back of his sister's seat, tapping the headrest with his toes, just to annoy the crap out of her.

This is Brian when he's stone-cold sober.

This is me with my heart crushed.

"Em, turn around, wouldja?" I tap the dashboard with the heel of my hand, startling Emily.

"What? What are you talking about?"

I have to go back. I'm not ready to leave her. "Bring me back to the hospital. Please?"

"But—"

"Please?"

She doesn't even look as she swings the Jeep around and does a U-turn, earning more than a few honks from other drivers. Ten long minutes later, we're back at the hospital.

"Don't wait for me. Just go home."

"What?" She pulls the Jeep over and idles at the curb. "How will you get back?"

"I'll figure it out." I hop out and bob my head at Brian. "Shotgun's all yours, dude." I cross in front of the car and stop at the driver's side. "Thanks, Em. You're an amazing friend."

She's stoic, as usual, because that's just who she is, but she reaches out for me and grabs me in a hug. "You're a good guy, Matty."

I take the hug. She waits until I head back toward the hospital before she drives off.

I didn't think I could do anything for Priya, but maybe I can.

She got me.

And I got her.

5:14 P.M.

The earlier part of the afternoon was such a whirlwind, my visit with Priya so brief, that I barely remember what happened.

Her face, so drawn and thin, that's what I remember, until her smile burst open wide and lit up the room. Her wispy black hair, not her platinum wig, I remember that, too.

But most of all I remember what wasn't there, what Emily didn't notice.

No life-saving machines. You don't have to be the son of a nurse to know what they look like, but if you've visited enough times, you kind of get to know the background hum.

And when it's not there, you notice. It wasn't a luxuriously appointed hospital room because it wasn't really a hospital room.

Priya is in hospice. She isn't at the hospital to get better. This is the end for her.

Or the beginning, depending on how you look at it. The field—my magic field—was Priya's beginning, her new adventure. And her parents took it away from her. But maybe I can give it back.

My father meets me at the hospital cafeteria about twenty minutes after I call him.

He spots me at once and his face splits into a happy grin. He practically runs to my table, shouting at me.

"Matty, you don't know how happy I was when you called," he says. "Gosh, I thought it was a dream or something."

I keep my distance, even as he throws his arms around my shoulders and hugs me. I haven't seen him in days, but it feels like a year. He's wearing a pair of khaki pants and a light blue collared shirt, and his normally unruly hair is plastered back into a helmet shape. He's got a backpack slung over one shoulder like he just stepped off a college campus. In other words, he looks very un-DJ-like. Must be Carol's influence.

"Look, this girl is . . ." How do I put this without betraying Priya? I don't want to tell my dad she thinks she's an alien. I don't want him to treat her like a lunatic, like I did.

"She's a big fan of the field."

"A new follower? I wonder if I know her. I just updated my blog after I moved here." He sounds eager and peppy, like he's bubbling over with optimism now that he's not living with me and Mom.

I try to cool his jets. "I just want you to talk to her, okay? Just tell her about the field or something. Nothing weird. No conspiracies or anything stupid."

"Sure, sure, I can do that," my dad says. He gestures toward the coffee bar at the front of the cafeteria. "How about I get us some coffees first, huh?"

"Uh, yeah, okay. Black, please."

"And two sugars, I know." He grins at me and hops up, adjusting his backpack as he goes. I feel like I'm being wooed on a first date by someone who *really* wants me to like him.

When he returns, he starts his spiel over again. I can feel it, like it's something he prepared on the drive over. "I'm glad you called me today, Junior."

Without looking at him, I say, "Could you call me Matty? Thanks."

"I know it might have been strange that I left in a hurry . . ."

I shrug and stare down into my coffee.

"I'd been thinking about it for a long time. It was never the right time."

When *is* the right time to leave your family? I wonder.

EIGHT DAYS ON PLANET EARTH

"So . . . Carol was the right time, huh?"

My dad's eyebrows knit in confusion. Did he *not* expect I would ask? "It was never about Carol. We were just friends. She wasn't happy and I wasn't happy. We left together but we're not *together*. Not like that."

"She's not at your new place?"

He scowls. "I don't know where she is." He slurps at his coffee and makes a face. "Not enough sugar."

"Always ask for two," I say like a wiseass.

He nods as if I'm brilliant or something, and we're silent for a moment.

"Your mom is amazing—"

"Don't say anything about Mom," I warn him.

"She did everything. Paid every bill. Made every decision. A long time ago she decided I was useless. She even tried to get me a job with my own brother."

I remember.

"But I wanted something else." He shakes his head. "Matty . . . I'm sorry."

I feel my pulse quicken. An apology. That's what I wanted, wasn't it? I search his face for deception, for insincerity, but see none. Instead I just see . . . a man.

Ordinary. Human.

He hesitates a moment and then, in a rush, says, "I understand if you hate me. I get it, I do. I'd probably hate me too."

I don't want to think about hating him, about forgiving

him—or not. I didn't ask him here for this.

"Dad? This is not the time."

I slurp my coffee, too much too soon, and scald the roof of my mouth. Whatever. I feel very whatever at this moment. I clear my throat dramatically, and in my head I hear the voice-over guy from *Real-Life Mystery*.

"Her name is Priya," I say. "And she believes she's an alien. . . ."

6:02 P.M.

When Dr. Shah opens the door to Priya's room, she frowns but then notices my dad and a peculiar look crosses her face.

My dad shoves his hand at her and turns on the charm. "Hello, I'm DJ Jones, Matthew's dad. I own the farm where your daughter was living for a few days."

She takes his hand slowly, a cool nonsmile on her face as she studies him. "Thank you for allowing our daughter to stay with you." She frowns until she finds the words that come next. "Our daughter. She . . . she followed you. Online?"

My father beams. His face is like a full moon.

"Dr. Shah, do you mind if we see Priya for a few minutes?" I ask. "My father has some information that might make Priya feel better. You know, calmer. I think we could be . . . helpful."

I hear a strangled sound come from the room, a muttered something and then *shhh*.

Dr. Shah glances behind her and nods and swings the door wide open. If I wasn't certain before, I definitely know now: the soft pink glow of light from the lamp, the subtle print on the cream-colored wallpaper, the cushioned recliners. Hospice.

Priya's in bed, arms stiff by her sides, eyes gazing up at the ceiling, just like she used to back at the field. Two white earbuds trail out of her ears and I wonder what she's listening to. It's so odd to see her with technology. She never had a phone or an iPod or a tablet in the time I knew her.

As I approach her, I notice something else: She looks . . . thinner.

Scary skinny.

Sick.

She's still beautiful. I remember her in the field, in my arms, against my body, in my bed. I remember her laughing at the kids at the lake, delighting in the soft fur of my dog, listening to the music of the trees.

Yes, she's still beautiful. She's not from another world, but she is special.

I tap her on the shoulder to get her attention. When she takes out her earbuds, I can hear her music, something light, a girl's high-pitched voice.

She sees me and grins happily. It's as if her earlier agitation never happened. She's the normal Priya.

"Matthew!" She pushes herself up to sitting and reaches a hand for me. I take a seat on her bed and kiss her cheek. Her parents probably won't like seeing that, but whatever.

"Priya, I want you to meet my dad, David Jones," I say as my dad comes forward.

"You can call me DJ."

Priya's hand, the one I'm not holding, covers her mouth as she giggles. "It's you! You were born the night the ship landed. I saw you online and on the tape Matthew showed me."

He nods, clearly thrilled she knows who he is. "I hear you came for a visit while I wasn't there."

"No, no, not a visit. My ship is coming for me." She starts to tremble, her voice anxious. "But I'm not there! How will I get home?"

I hold my breath as I watch the inner workings of my dad's mind play out on his face. What will he tell her? The truth? Whose truth—his or the rest of the world's?

"I think you might have miscalculated the landing area," my dad says finally.

Priya's eyebrows knit. "No, that's the field. I know it is."

"You are traveling by wormhole, yes?"

"Yes, but this wormhole is stable. It's one of only a hundred and fifteen that we know of that are stable at both ends."

If this throws my father off, he doesn't show it. He holds up a finger. "Very true, but did you consider the Earth's position in space will be different from where it was over fifty years ago? The wormhole may have a stable exit point, but where will the Earth be in relation to it?"

He sounds so confident that I wonder if it's real science or science fiction. I glance at the Shahs, who are *not* disagreeing, although at this point, I think they would let anyone talk to their daughter if it meant keeping her happy.

Damn if my dad doesn't sound like he knows his shit.

I wait to see if Priya buys it.

Slowly, very slowly, it sinks in and she smiles. "You're right! I didn't figure that into my calculations."

My father looks visibly relieved. "Well, let's take a look at your calculations, then."

Priya responds with renewed enthusiasm and more happy energy than I've seen since she was at the field. "My notebook is in my bag." She looks around the room, but I spot it first and retrieve it.

My father slings his backpack off his shoulder and shows her that he too has a black bag. Don't all great space travelers? "I carry a notebook too, but it's electronic."

I expect her to hold fast to the notebook in her hand, but

she gladly shows my father her precious.

As he carefully—reverently—turns the pages, I catch more of the scribbles she made during her visit. Her handwriting in the final pages is sloppy and inconsistent and I can barely make out many words, but I do see . . .

Matthew.

Ginger.

Love.

I feel my cheeks grow warm and I wonder if my dad sees those words too. If he does, he says nothing. "Okay, here we go. Look at this formula you have," he says, pointing to a series of equations. "Explain this one to me."

While Priya eagerly reasons out her calculations, I glance back at the Shahs, who are obviously enthralled by the effect my dad is having on their daughter.

Both my dad and Priya are exactly who they want to be, right in this moment. And they are blissful.

"Tell me more about the field, DJ," I hear Priya say. "What was it like to live so close to it for all your life?"

My father looks over at me, includes me with his smile. "Why don't I let Matty tell you?"

"Huh, me? But I—"

"Remember how we used to set up our telescopes side by side out in the field?" he asks me. "We'd bring out sandwiches and cans of soda, which your mother hated, said you'd rot your teeth."

"Oh yeah, that's right." I do remember that. "Mom would tell me to drink more milk instead. She can be such a nurse sometimes."

Priya grins and settles into her pillows like a kid being told a bedtime story. "Please tell me more."

"You want to tell her why the field was the perfect place for stargazing?" my dad prompts.

"Because there are no obstructions. No trees, no power lines, no tall buildings . . . not even any streetlamps," I say automatically as I put myself back in the field next to my dad.

"It's the ideal place to search the sky."

A flash of a computer screen, my dad's ugly website, pops into my mind. Images of the two of us at our telescopes, photos I remember my mom taking back when it was all-science-all-the-time for DJ and Junior. And under each photo my dad posted was a comment:

I'm so proud of Matthew learning how to find Orion on his own.

Matthew is going to be a great astronomer someday!

Matthew and I are going to sleep in the field tonight so we can watch for the comet.

Posing for photos with my telescope, my finger pointed toward the night sky and my face filled with awe, I looked like Boy Astronomer.

"The comet!" I say. "Do you remember?" It was June 2010. A new comet was headed our way. A fuzzy green ball in the sky, bigger and more clearly visible than so many that came before it.

"Yes!" My dad bobs his head. "We set our alarm clocks so we could get up just about an hour before sunrise."

Our spot in that wide-open field, far from light pollution, was almost as good as being at an observatory. We could have seen it with binoculars, but with our telescopes, we were up-close and personal with the two-tailed comet.

Even recalling it now is thrilling. Out in the field alone, we could imagine ourselves as famous astronomers, as if *we* were the ones discovering it.

I feel Priya's hand clasp mine and I glance up; her right hand holds my dad's. The three of us, connected.

"I remember that comet too," she says.

"It disappeared after that summer," my dad says. "Gone from our solar system."

"From ours, as well," Priya says.

Gone. Disappeared. A final flight. A last hurrah. Comet C2009/R1 spun past us in a showy dazzle of light and left us permanently.

"Those bright green tails," my dad says. "Remember, Junior?"

"How could I forget? It was amazing!"

"Better than the best episode of the original series," Dad teases. He always did like Captain Kirk better than Picard.

We both turn to Priya, who regards us intently. She

gazes first at me and then at my dad. "Resistance is futile," she says robotically. Just. Like. A. Borg.

I whoop with delight. "Yes! I knew you were a Next Gen fan." I squeeze her fingers between mine and enjoy seeing my dad wince.

He casts an eye at the Shahs, one eyebrow raised as if to say, *I can't believe I spawned this.*

"*Star Trek* was part of my vast data collection," Priya says.

Behind us, the door opens and a nurse enters with a tray. "Did someone order pizza for dinner?" she asks with a grin.

"Did you?" I ask Priya, and she nods.

"I love pizza."

I hear *I love you*, but I know that's not what she said.

Priya's father clears his throat. "Matthew, perhaps you'll leave now and come back tomorrow."

"Visiting hours begin at ten," the nurse adds helpfully and pointedly.

"Oh yeah, yeah, of course," I say, even though I'm nowhere near ready to go. I bend down to hug Priya and she kisses me on the lips, her face melting into mine, a long, lingering kiss that feels . . . final.

I press my fingers into her back and hold her tightly against my chest, feel her lips against my neck and her eyelashes brushing my cheek. *Don't cry, Matty, don't you fucking cry now.*

"Everything will be okay." I hear her voice lightly in my ear. "You must believe."

"I do," I whisper. "I do believe."

When we part, she smiles at my dad. "Thank you, DJ. I'm so grateful you helped me with my calculations."

"It was my pleasure. If I don't see you again, I wish you . . . safe travels." My father blinks and looks away and I swear he's swallowing hard.

When we say good night to the Shahs, I can feel their gratitude. Even if they don't say it out loud.

It's like, yeah, I can read their minds.

Out on the street, I walk my dad to his truck and shake his hand, formally. "Thanks for coming. That really helped her," I say.

"Oh, um, yeah, no worries at all," he says. "Hey, how are you getting home?"

I hadn't thought about that much. "The bus?"

"A bus? Tonight?" His voice is coated in doubt.

"Well, yeah, I guess. . . ." But it does sound silly, especially if I'm just coming back in the morning. "Maybe I'll try to sneak a sleepover at the hospital," I say.

My dad doesn't acknowledge my dumb idea but instead says, "How about a bite to eat and then you can go home?"

Food. Now, who's gonna turn down free food?

"I know a good pizza joint that delivers," Dad says. "We could watch *Trek* while we eat."

"*Next Gen*?" I suggest.

But my dad is adamant. "Not in my house. It's Kirk and Spock or nothing."

I don't take too long to decide. "Yeah, okay."

My dad looks like he just won the lottery. Or discovered his own comet. "Hop in. You want cheese and mushrooms?"

"And sausage and pepperoni."

"My kind of pie."

I slide into the passenger side of the truck and feel a familiarity to our positions. Me and Dad, side by side, just like being in the field. I glance up through the windshield, wave a silent good-bye to Priya in her room, eating her pizza.

"Looks like I might be getting a job at the observatory here in Philly," my dad says as he pulls away from the curb.

We are ready at last to set sail for the stars.

That's one of my dad's favorite Carl Sagan quotes.

DAY EIGHT

9:43 A.M.

So I didn't take the bus home. Turns out Dad had the entire original series on DVD so we had to binge. Plus there was the pizza.

He pulls the truck up to the curb outside the hospital and slides it into park. We both get out of the car and I feel tension string between us like a live wire.

Before he can say thank you or whatever, I blurt out, "I don't hate you."

My dad's face opens in surprise. "Okay. Good."

"I don't . . . I don't like you right now. I don't like how you did what you did, but I . . ." The words don't sound right.

They don't come smoothly or easily. "I miss you. I miss hanging out with you."

I shove my hands into my pockets. I can feel my face grow warm—from the sun, definitely the sun—and I have to look away. "I miss how things were when I was a kid and we did stuff together."

I didn't realize just how much I'd missed him—us—until Priya stepped into my life.

"Yeah, me too. But it happens. You have school and friends. And I probably embarrassed the heck out of you." He half laughs; we both know the truth of that statement.

"Well, I guess . . ." I didn't understand. I didn't know. *Think like a cat.* I didn't think like DJ Jones at all. I only thought like me.

I feel a hitch in my throat. "I don't like people leaving. Priya, Em . . . you."

He doesn't say anything, doesn't contradict me. He's not coming back. Em's going away. So is Priya.

I'm right. For once, I'm not a step behind everyone else. And it sucks.

I feel my chest sink, my heart drop into my stomach. I lean on the truck, rest my head on my arms; the roof of the pickup, warmed by the sun, sears my skin.

I feel my dad's hand on my back and his breath in my ear. "From the moment we're born, we're dying, Matty. We're just like the stars. We burst into life and then slowly burn out. It's up to you to make the light shine brightest and longest."

I turn my head to look at him.

"That's what your granddad told me on the night I was born."

"You can't possibly remember that."

"It's the only thing I *do* remember him saying."

I can't help but laugh through my tears. "You're special, all right."

We stand together, looking up at the hospital. I try to imagine Priya and her parents having coffee together. I make a mental note to grab some doughnuts from the cafeteria before I go up.

"You gonna be okay by yourself?" Dad asks.

"Yeah, I'm fine."

He taps the phone that's in his back pocket and says, "You know how to reach me."

We don't hug. We're not huggers in the Jones family.

Just before he walks away, my dad grabs me in an awkward embrace.

Okay. I guess we're huggers now.

Inside the hospital, sunbeams scatter my path as I walk across the linoleum. The whole place feels brighter, more welcoming than the day before.

I get in line for my visitor's pass with a smile.

"I'm here to see Priya Shah," I say cheerfully. Her name

sounds so delicate and pretty. How could you not smile when you say it?

The receptionist behind the desk pauses with her fingers held above her keyboard. Her gaze meets mine briefly and then flickers away.

"I'm sorry, but . . ."

5:36 P.M.

I imagine her alive, tilting her head to one side, not understanding my fear because of course she has to go, of course
she can't be here anymore. Her job is done. She has collected all the data she needs. Her visit is over and she's
being called back home.

I want to tell her, *Don't leave me.*

I want to tell her, *My life won't be the same without you.*

I want to tell her . . .

I love you, for what you've brought me.

I love you, for what you've brought back to me.

But she's gone.

"Safe travels," I whisper.

9:59 P.M.

Out in the field, the telescope is in the same spot where I left it and so is the tent. I should probably bring both of them inside in case it rains. But I can't.

I keep thinking she's going to come back. She's going to traipse up the hill with her black bag and her white wig. Ginger will bark until I let her out, and she'll dash under the willows and across the creek to bury her fat head under Priya's hand.

So I have to leave it there, trained on the night sky, deep into the constellation Libra where a small planet near Gliese 581c orbits its sun twenty light-years from Earth.

I close my eyes and put myself back in Priya's room, locking eyes with her and listening to her mom talk to Emily.

Astrocytoma. Dr. Shah said she'd had the tumors since she was a girl. Surgery. Radiation. Hard to remove.

Back at Dad's apartment, while he dozed after pizza and *Star Trek*, I opened his tablet and threw some words into a search engine. Astrocytoma means brain tumor. Called "astro" because they're shaped like stars.

I scanned the page for signs and symptoms and found:

Poor hand-eye coordination.

I recalled how she cried when she accidentally grabbed Ginger's tail instead of petting her.

Difficulty standing or walking.

"I am not used to your gravity," Priya had said when her knees collapsed under her.

Memory lapses.

Her notebook. *Red means stop, my name is Priya,* and on and on in her "data collection" book. She'd forgotten how to swim. She didn't know what a dog was. She sometimes didn't recognize me. She forgot her own parents.

I'd assumed the struggles she had to find words were due to a language barrier, but that was just one more symptom of her deteriorating condition.

Another medical website told me that tumors often press on different parts of the brain, causing reactions that no one can predict. Not everything is mapped out.

Does reading another person's mind count as an unpredictable reaction? We were connected, Priya and me. She knew what I was thinking, what I wanted, what I was feeling.

She got me.

But the field . . .

I feel a sudden anger burning inside me, claiming space in my chest, sucking all the air out of my lungs. "Why be an alien? Why not just be a girl who likes space?"

But that's not what it was about.

Like my dad, Priya found something to believe in in the field. She found solace in the knowledge that we are not alone in the Universe.

Astrocytoma. I roll the word around in my head. For a girl who loves space, who loves science, it was fate perhaps that she had an entire constellation in her body and soul.

A girl who doesn't want to die . . . maybe she finds a way to not be a girl.

Ginger, patient at my heels, whines as if she knows Priya's really gone. I reach a hand down to pet her and she responds with a nuzzle for more.

With my eye to the telescope, I search the skies. Is that a shooting star? The tail of a comet? Or the flare from the back of a rocket? I imagine Priya on her ship back to her home planet, whooshing through the wormhole that somehow reminds her of eating a pizza.

A grin spreads across my face.

Stars scatter the sky like jewels and for a moment, I think I really can see Priya's home planet. It's the one that shines the brightest, glows the longest.

I'm not ready to go back to the house, to my normal life. Not yet. I want to feel the Universe around me, surround me, blanket me.

I tap the screen on my phone to get the flashlight app, but in the low light I can't see what I'm touching and manage to open the camera roll instead.

There's a video on it that I didn't take.

The hair on the back of my neck is electrified and my heart beats faster. Just like the night I met Priya in this very field. The night leaves swirled around her and her laugh teased the air. *She* was the one who made this field magical.

It's Priya on my phone.

"Hello, Matthew," she says to the camera. "Thank you for the use of your phone."

She took my cell that night, swiped it from my kitchen while I slept.

"I have no need to call anyone, of course. They are on their way very soon. As I speak these words, they are on their way to me. They want me back and I want to be back."

I touch the screen, pausing it for a moment so I can

study her face. Did I miss something in the words she said, the way she said them?

I press play.

"Please take care of your dog. I sense that she needs much more affection than you give her."

I glance over at Ginger. That's not hard to figure out.

"Thank you for taking care of this field, Matthew. I sense that you will miss me when I'm gone but you should not. I have collected all the data that I need." Her gaze flits away from the camera and I hear her sigh before she looks back at the camera—at me—again. "I have enjoyed my time on Earth."

The video ends abruptly. Just fifteen seconds long. I play it again and again and again. It doesn't get any longer. It doesn't say anything more than that.

I feel a fresh wave of tears wash over me. I thought I was done at the hospital. Or on the bus ride home from Philly. Or in my mom's arms earlier tonight.

My time on Earth. Our brief blip of time. A sliver of incandescence in the vast, dark field of space.

When my dad and Carol left, I flippantly told my mom that the ones left behind need to get on with their lives. How can we? How can *I*?

I don't know what the future holds. For me. For my mom. For my dad. Priya taught me in just a few days that even if you can't see something, you can believe in it. Whether that's life on another planet, faith in a god we can't see, or simply love, it doesn't need to be proved to exist in order for your heart to know that it does.

We are part of this Universe; we are in this Universe, but perhaps more important than both of those facts is that the Universe is in us.

—*Neil deGrasse Tyson*

ACKNOWLEDGMENTS

This book is very close to my heart, and so are the people who have supported and encouraged me along the way.

To my editor, Kristen Pettit: thank you for always pushing me to take my characters deeper and expose them to the world, for showing me nuance and shading, and for plucking things from my brain I didn't know were there.

To my agent, Adam Peck: thank you for your enthusiasm, your detailed critiques, and your ongoing mentorship. I am happiest when I know you love something.

To Jen Klonsky and Elizabeth Lynch at HarperTeen: thank you for your continued support of me and my work, both virtually and in the real world. And to the marketing and publicity teams at HarperCollins: thank you for helping my book reach readers around the world.

To my beta readers, Omaira Galarza, Corey McCullough, and Gwen Owens: thank you for cheering me on from the book's earliest drafts.

To astronomer April P. Senjo: thank you for vetting the science in my fiction and for helping me align the stars.

To copy editor Brenna Franzitta and production editor Renée Cafiero: thank you both for your razor-sharp attention to detail and insistence on clarity.

To Sarah Kaufman, the book's cover designer: thank you for making my jaw drop. Your beautiful art stuns me.

To my mom and dad: thank you for reading and loving this book. It was written for you, for us, for where we came from. It was written with love.

To my husband: thank you for always saying, "You did a great job," when you know I need to hear that.

And finally, to you, my readers: thank you for taking the time to read this book, for inviting Matty and Priya into your lives for a little while.

We are all stars. We are all the stuff of the Universe.

#ibelieve